# MAHAVEER

**Rupa Srikumar** is a poet, translator and novelist. She has also written for the radio and the stage. With her husband A.K. Srikumar, she has translated Yasmin Khalid Rafi's *Mohammad Rafi: My Abba – A Memoir* from Hindi to English. Her radio plays have been broadcast by AIR. Her adaptation of Jai Shankar Prasad's Hindi play *Ajatasatru* was staged in Delhi University some years ago. *Mahaveer* is Rupa's first novel.

**A.K. Srikumar** is a novelist, translator, poet and playwright. Srikumar also writes fiction for children. Most of his children's books have won first or second places in the annual competition of the Children's Book Trust. *Operation Polo* (1997) was adjudged the 'Best Children's Book of the Year'. He has authored *The Wonderful World of Nilayam Swamy* (1981), *Conversations with a Motor-cycle* (1984), and the historical novel, *The Begum's Secret* (2010), which was long-listed for the Vodafone-Crossword Literary Prize. His play *Bhishma* was staged in Ahmedabad. Srikumar's English translation of T.V. Varkey's Malayalam classic *Maanju Pokunna Thalamurakal* (The Vanishing Generations) was published in September 2017.

A.K. Srikumar and Rupa live in Mumbai.

# MAHAVEER

## *the* Soldier *who* Never Died

RUPA SRIKUMAR & A.K. SRIKUMAR

RUPA

*To our parents*

Published by
Rupa Publications India Pvt. Ltd 2019
7/16, Ansari Road, Daryaganj
New Delhi 110002

*Sales centres:*
Allahabad Bengaluru Chennai
Hyderabad Jaipur Kathmandu
Kolkata Mumbai



ISBN: 978-93-5333-629-5

First impression 2019

10 9 8 7 6 5 4 3 2 1

Printed at HT Media Ltd, Gr. Noida

# I

'What do you know about the Sumdorong Chu?'

Lieutenant Akash Sinha met his Adjutant's quizzical gaze with a blank expression. He was talking about the Sumdorong–McMahon Line incident. But as the penny dropped and he opened his mouth to speak, Major Bhagwani continued, 'I'm not talking about classroom lectures. I know they told you about that eighties' incident, when the Chinese crossed the McMahon line, along the river, and we pushed them back. Those Chinese shat their pants when they saw we meant business.'

Akash recalled the episode as discussed in one of his classes at the Indian Military Academy. He also remembered that the Major's reading of the situation wasn't entirely correct. The Chinese had not, as the Adjutant put it, 'shat their pants'. Actually, both nations had decided that escalation of the conflict wasn't worth their while, and had agreed to withdraw simultaneously to their respective positions before the alleged infraction. However, Akash knew better than to be drawn into an argument with his superior. He simply nodded, 'Yes, Sir,' wondering what he had done to incur the 2i/c's displeasure.

As if in answer to his unspoken thought, the Major looked askance at the Lieutenant while still seeming engrossed in the papers on his desk.

'We've received intelligence inputs recently...about some movements near the Thandrong pasture. That's where the Chinese crossed over and set up bunkers on our side of the line, back in the eighties. HQ fears the enemy might be trying something similar, again. But we have regular patrols out there, and we certainly don't think so. Still, the CO has decided that we ought to check it out. Of course, in my opinion, they're only rumours...and these chaps from Intelligence often get it wrong. But...orders are orders.'

'Yes, Sir,' Akash clicked his heels.

'I'm sending a patrol out there. It will have to be after nightfall, of course,' the Major's eyes appeared to scrutinize his subordinate's face, as if for telltale signs of any reaction. By now, Akash knew better than to react. Bhagwani continued, 'It will take some brave men...and officers...to go out there.'

Akash saluted once more, 'Lieutenant Akash Sinha seeking permission to volunteer for patrol detail, Sir.'

'And yes, you'll have your infra technology and GPS to help you at the border, Lieutenant. That's what you millennials swear by, eh? The Subedar will tell you how we use that stuff out here.'

Twelve hours later, the Lieutenant was wondering whether he had made the right decision by precipitately volunteering for this task. He hadn't even had time to get acclimatized to life on the border.

The valley of the Sumdorong rivulet, along the McMahon Line, is a different world. It is at no great distance from Tawang, barely 50 kilometres, but that proximity is no comfort. As far as

Akash and his patrol were concerned, brigade headquarters might have been a thousand miles away. Besides, days and nights in the mountains are worlds apart. The sunlight is salubrious; some might say reminiscent of heaven on earth. Even work can seem like pleasure, despite the constant struggle for oxygen at the great heights. And then there is the restful, brilliant green of forest, clothing mountainsides beneath blue sky, like a mother's embrace.

Nights, on the other hand, can seem like a different planet. Pitch dark. Familiar roads become unknown and treacherous for the uninitiated, with the silence of the tomb and no living soul, human or even animal, out in the freezing cold during those hours. All that can be seen, when there is any kind of visibility, are towering, snow-covered peaks—as if they were peeping out of the enveloping dark only to sneer at the puny human beings with the temerity to venture among them. The whine of the bone-chilling breeze is all the sound one hears in the night. For a newcomer, it can be dreadful.

The noises and bustle of the metropolis, the blinding illumination that lights up the night in a city—Lieutenant Sinha could not help recalling all that he had left behind, less than a week ago. He was still preoccupied with these thoughts as the compact party of daredevils trudged along in the desolate night towards the pasture where the Chinese movements had been spotted, according to the intelligence reports the Adjutant had shared with him.

So, despite the Major's taunt, Akash was glad they had GPS and night vision.

Akash's platoon moved in absolute silence. They would be patrolling close to Chinese bunkers. There was to be no conversation unless warranted, and no calling out, and radio silence had to be maintained.

Subedar Gurung was leading with an advance section, because he had spent time in these parts and knew the place almost like the back of his hand, to the extent that anyone can understand nature. The JCO was following the coordinates provided by intel.

When at first Akash heard the hissing in his ears, a couple of hours into the patrol, he thought it was a breeze. But then he realized the night was still, and the air itself was holding its breath in this cold night. So, what was…there it was again—the buzzing. He stopped in midstride, and the Havildar and jawan following him almost crashed into him.

He turned quickly to look at his companions with an apologetic gaze. Their eyes burned like embers in the night, with the obvious question which they could not utter, for fear of breaking the silence. 'What is it, Saabji…' he could see the question on the Havildar's darkened face, but then the hissing in his ear was distinct now, as if someone were speaking to him.

Speaking? There was someone talking to him, but his colleagues' lips were sealed, he was sure. They knew better than to create sound in the stillness. So, who was telling him, 'That way, turn left here, left…'

Turn left? But if he did that they would break away from the direction Subedar Gurung was leading them towards.

The hesitation of a few moments had already cost them, putting distance between the advance party and Akash's group. In the darkness that could be dangerous, even fatal.

'That way, turn left here…' the disembodied voice was insistent now.

As if sensing what was happening, the Havildar, a grizzled veteran, sidled up to Akash, murmuring, 'Do you want to go that way, Sir? Is that it?'

'No, no!' Akash protested, 'It's this...crazy...I should just ignore it. Let's keep moving; follow the GPS...'

'No, Sir. I think I know what it is. That's the direction we will go, if...' the Havildar left the rest unsaid, but Akash understood what he meant.

The rest of his men hesitated, as if waiting for the Lieutenant to make up his mind. Then Akash pointed into the dark, signalling to his section that they should go on, while he turned left here. He gestured to the Havildar to join him.

For a moment more the men balked, wondering, probably, about the wisdom of deviating from the course set by the Subedar. But then, discipline triumphed and Akash could see a couple of them shaking their heads in apparent dismay before they headed off in the direction Subedar Gurung had taken, letting the rookie Lieutenant and the Havildar investigate this new lead.

Wisely, Akash let the Havildar lead. The non-com was a veteran. Soon, the Lieutenant could sense that they were walking through rock and reeds, which could mean that they were approaching the river. Progressing silently became that much more difficult. Akash was beginning to wonder whether his hunch had been little more than foolishness, that voice a chimera, now that they were well and truly out of range of Subedar Gurung's group.

Then he sensed rather than saw the Havildar halt. The non-com glanced over his shoulder at the Lieutenant, and pointed wordlessly. Akash crept closer, trying to make as little noise as possible among the reeds.

It was unmistakable—the sound of voices. A minute longer and they could see a faint glow through the vegetation, perhaps light bouncing off surrounding rock. It was a moonless night, so the lights had to be...man made.

'Enemy, Saabji,' the Havildar whispered, taking a chance.

Akash nodded and signalled, as if asking whether they should split up, so they could pincer whoever was out there, near those lights. Without doubt, the unknowns were on the Indian side of the line, and they were certainly not an Indian patrol. Of that even he was certain.

Low voices were now audible as they approached the area. Protected as they were by the dark and cold, their quarry certainly didn't seem to entertain any apprehensions of being surprised.

But even as the thought occurred to him, he realized there was a problem. Close to ten metres of open space separated Akash and his companion from the strangers. The Havildar signalled. There were two men out there. Which evened the odds, of course.

Then the Lieutenant made a decision, and hefted his automatic rifle. Lifting it to his shoulder and pointing the barrel at the still unaware intruders, he began to walk forward, calling aloud, '*Kaun hai?* Who's there?' Out of the corner of one eye, he could see the Havildar follow his lead, moving off to the left as he advanced so that they would catch the enemy—if such they were—in a pincer if the situation warranted. But it turned out that they needn't have worried. Alerted by Akash's shout, two figures got slowly to their feet, with arms lifted, speaking in a dialect.

'They're herders, Saabji,' said the Havildar, hoarsely. 'I know their type—yak herders. Look at their clothes.'

'No, look at their features. They could be Chinese for all we know. Ask them what they're doing here at this hour so close to the border.'

The Havildar conveyed his officer's question in a mixture of Hindi and Monpa, and when they replied, he turned to Akash, pointing, 'They are yak herders, Saabji, not Chinese. Monpa herders...of that I'm certain.'

As if to confirm the strangers' inoffensive antecedents, the Lieutenant's gaze followed the Havildar's pointing finger, and he was able to make out the bulk of a couple of the herbivores, hunkered down in the night a few feet from where the men were warming themselves around a fire.

'They say there is some fine grazing out here. During daytime, the Chinese threaten them if they find them here. So they take a chance and bring their yaks during the night occasionally.'

'Is that so?' Akash shrugged, lowering his rifle, 'Well...they should be glad we didn't shoot them at sight. How do we know they aren't spies?'

'We don't, Saabji. But the Monpas live in these parts. They own these mountains, more or less. There's very little we can do to stop them moving about as they please.'

'That's so much time wasted, then...' growled Akash, and turned away from the intruders. But as he did, a glimmer struck his eyes, and in the moment that it did, he realized that it was the gleam of light falling on metal. Steel. Even in the shadow of the rock against which it leaned, his trained eyes could make out the contours of an automatic rifle.

The Havildar also had turned around, and had already stepped ahead of Akash. A loud click sounded behind them. The Lieutenant could not quite decide afterwards whether it was the same voice that had brought them here, which impelled him to look in the direction of the concealed weapon. But at this moment his reaction was instantaneous, without a thought. In one smooth, fluid motion, he whirled, cocking his rifle even as his trigger finger curled around the rigid steel and pulled it.

There was only a single burst of gunfire, and it caught one of the Monpas in the chest, sending him staggering back and his weapon clattering on the rocks. The other man lunged for the rifle concealed behind the rock, and he would have scooped it up, if the Havildar's flying tackle hadn't pinned him to the ground, inches short of his weapon. In a moment, the veteran soldier was all over the supposed Monpa, punching the man unconscious with his terrible fists.

'Let's tie him up and take him with us,' said Akash, having ascertained that his target was beyond any aid. The burst from the Lieutenant's rifle had been fatal.

There was still the problem of finding their way towards the rest of the platoon, thought Akash, as the two men trudged silently back after the successful encounter. The burly Havildar carried their captive in a fireman's lift, to ensure that the man had no chance of slipping away into the surrounding darkness, if he regained consciousness any time soon.

But they needn't have worried about getting lost. Subedar Gurung had dealt with lost details and missing soldiers earlier. As soon as he realized that Akash and his section were not bringing up the rear as they were supposed to, the veteran of many such night patrols had the good sense to return and look for his Lieutenant. It was another matter that he made no effort to hide his displeasure at the risk Akash had taken in the darkness, given the Lieutenant's inexperience of the wilderness or of actual combat.

'It was my fault,' Akash felt obliged to reply, seeing the unspoken query in the Junior Commissioned Officer's (JCO) eyes, 'Going by gut instinct rather than actual intel…'

'We have a prisoner, Saabji,' the Havildar reminded.

'You should've killed the bastard,' grated the Subedar, 'Why do we need to carry him back to Brigade? He's either Chinese… or a Monpa spy.'

'Oh, no…if he is a spy, the man may have information.'

At which point the Havildar stepped up to the JCO and whispered something into his ears. Watching, Akash could make out, even in the indistinct light, the dawning comprehension upon Gurung's face.

'So *that* is what happened?'

'What…what are you talking about?' Akash snapped, irritable and tired by now. The action had taken a toll on his body and nerves.

'Nothing like this has come to pass in a long time, Saabji,' said the Subedar, looking into the distance. 'It seems he has chosen you.'

That Lieutenant Akash Sinha did not feel like the chosen one, at the debriefing with the Adjutant, was another matter.

'This is insubordination, Lieutenant,' the Major snarled, and then hastily changed his tone to a silken threat, 'You know what happens when people don't follow orders in the army…'

Akash might have told his superior that he hadn't actually disobeyed instructions. All he did was follow his gut, and as a result they now had a prisoner, which was much better than going by unsubstantiated intel reports. There was also no point mentioning his Havildar's role in the decision. So, he said nothing, choosing discretion rather than conversation with an angry boss under the circumstances.

But Bhagwani wasn't to be denied. As if reading the Lieutenant's mind, he said scathingly, 'Whatever came over you, Lieutenant...wandering off like that on a whim...a...an imaginary whisper...that's what it was, wasn't it?'

'Er...yes, Sir. But, the jawans believe me, Sir. Even the... Subedar. Gurung said...'

'I can imagine what Subedar Gurung might have told you, Lieutenant. Now look here, these myths about martyrs and their ghosts...they are all very well for the jawans. They are not educated beyond high school—most of them—and they're superstitious. But you and I, we're officers, Lieutenant Sinha. Remember that. We must look at every situation in the cold light of reason, not flights of fancy. Or...or whispers in the dark. And you're an engineer...or have you forgotten that too?'

'But...it turned out to be correct, Sir. We did locate the intruders. And we got a prisoner, too.'

'Ha! That prisoner you brought in...do you know who those men were?'

'Spies, probably...' Akash wanted to say, but opted for a murmured 'No, Sir.'

'Just herders, that's what they are...were...Monpa yak herders, that is who they were. These men live in the mountains around us, and they can go anywhere at any time. They are also citizens of this country, Lieutenant Akash Sinha. We cannot go around killing our own people, understand? Their lives aren't cheap because they are only poor, unarmed shepherds caught in the crossfire between countries.'

Although Akash tried to look contrite, something in the Major's diatribe had caught his attention. So he made bold to ask, 'Er...they had weapons, Sir. And I intend to question the prisoner, Sir, to find out what the two of them were doing out there at that time of night.'

'That won't be necessary, Lieutenant,' Akash thought he noticed just a shade of tension in the Adjutant's words. 'We already did. He knows nothing. The yak herders carry them sometimes for self-defence against the Chinese, just in case they wander too close to the Line. That's no proof that they were spies…we had to let him go.'

'But, Sir…you mean… we went to all that trouble…'

'What I mean, Lieutenant, is that you overstepped, and made a hash of your first real task. Well, I don't blame you. Delhi thinks they can send anyone out here, even a wet-behind-the-ears engineer who thinks technology can replace real soldiers…and find out what we haven't been able to, with all our experience and resources. Now just pray that the yak herder doesn't raise a hue and cry about the treatment meted out to him. That Havildar of yours bashed him up badly, and you killed his comrade. This could have political ramifications, you know?'

As Akash left the Adjutant's office, he was shaken, and possessed by a sense of extreme guilt. Somehow, despite the fact it was a legitimate military action against unidentified intruders on a disputed international border, he couldn't help thinking that he was in some way responsible for the yak herder's pointless death. He had also risked the life of a colleague in what, ultimately, had become an exercise in futility.

Even the commendations he received from some of his peers in the battalion's mess late that evening did little to dispel Akash's creeping sense of guilt.

'Great action, Akash,' a couple of them said.

Others patted his back, saying, 'Don't mind Bhagu. He's always whining about anything we do. We're on to him, most of us, so he decided to pick on you.'

It was in a highly contemplative frame of mind that Akash retired to bed later that night. For one thing, he had seen action. As for Bhagwani's warning about 'political ramifications', the Lieutenant couldn't even begin to think on those lines. He was a soldier not a politician.

# 2

When the Adjutant called him into his office the following day, Akash thought he might receive his transfer orders out of Tawang—which might not be such a bad thing—or another dressing down, at the least. Instead, Major Bhagwani invited him to sit down.

'Read that,' he said, pushing a piece of paper across the table towards the Lieutenant.

Akash picked it up and looked at the letterhead. 'Association of Gram Panchayats of Tawang,' it said in English, alongside the Hindi version, as in Government of India stationery.

'What…is this, Sir?'

'Just read the letter first,' said the Major, curtly.

The contents were in stilted, rather officious English. As Akash read on, he became more and more confused by the contents of the letter, and even more so as to what this had to do with him.

'It seems like a representation from all the gram panchayats of Tawang, Sir,' he said, looking up after he had finished reading. 'Something about a couple of Monpa girls…and a memorial to them…etcetera. But, Sir…this is addressed to Brigade Headquarters…with copies to Army Headquarters and the

Ministry of Home...'

'That's right,' Bhagwani nodded, 'That is exactly what it is. Now, you're wondering what this has to do with you, aren't you?'

'I beg your pardon, Sir. But that had occurred to me, Sir.'

'Well, I'll put it to you this way,' the Major got up and started to pace up and down, appearing to focus on the trophy cabinet that lined the wall behind his chair. 'If it hadn't been for you, Lieutenant...ahem, what happened out there on the Thandrong Pasture a couple of nights ago, this would have nothing to do with you. It is an administrative issue...political, actually, and quite outside the competence of even Brigade to decide upon.'

'Yes, Sir.' Akash tried not to look mystified.

'Now, as I said earlier, these Monpas are simple people, quite pious and not very educated. So are most of our jawans, fortunately or unfortunately. What that means is that they are quite gullible people.'

'Well...er...maybe so, Sir.'

'You can take this from me, education makes a huge difference, Lieutenant. Take yourself for instance...do you really believe that it was a ghost whispering to you that night...eh?'

'I...well...I don't really know, Sir. Now I think it was my... er...sixth sense, Sir.'

'Exactly what I think, too. But many people hereabouts have a different view of the matter. You have heard of the Baba... of Jaswantgarh?'

'Jaswant Singh Rawat, MVC? Of course I have, Sir. Everybody in the army has, I think, Sir.'

'In that case, you may also be aware of the myth that has taken root over the past several decades...' Bhagwani leaned across the table, looking straight at Akash.

'What…myth…Sir?'

'About a couple of Monpa girls that are rumoured to have helped the Baba…I mean Rifleman Jaswant Singh Rawat, when he made his last stand at Nuranang.'

'I might have heard, Sir. I don't remember…'

'Well, then…it's time to jostle your memory,' the Major sat down again, picked up the letter and gazed fixedly at it. 'As you have read, this is a representation, presumably from the people of Tawang, seeking a memorial for those Monpa girls, who they claim helped Rifleman Jaswant Singh Rawat in the battle of Nuranang.'

'That's right, Sir. That is what it seems to be, Sir. But I don't understand…'

'You don't understand what this has to do with you, or that night's goof-up, eh?'

'Well, yes Sir.'

'Neither Army HQ nor the Ministry of Home Affairs were inclined to take this representation very seriously, you see. Not immediately, anyway. They have been seeing it more as a gimmick by local politicians with an axe to grind, than any real popular sentiment.'

'That may be, Sir.'

'Not any more, Lieutenant.' Major Bhagwani tapped his glass tabletop with one forefinger, 'That herder's death has set off a political storm of sorts. So, the only way the higher-ups see to handle this is to tell the public here that we are considering this long-pending request in deference to their sentiments. You know how these things work…'

'I…actually don't, Sir.'

'Of course you don't, Lieutenant. You're still a novice. Let me explain. Here is how this will pan out. As of now, you are officially in charge of the Army's "Operation Sadbhavana" in Tawang.'

'What's...that, Sir?'

'Local outreach, my friend. Pure and simple public relations. You will meet the people, talk to them, visit Jaswantgarh and investigate what happened in 1962 at Nuranang...'

'But...how can I...investigate anything, Sir?'

'Of course you can't, son. But you have to go through the rigmarole. After a reasonable interval, you will submit a report, based on which the Brigade will send a memorandum to Sena Bhawan explaining why creating a memorial for such mythical personalities may serve no worthwhile purpose, and may only open a Pandora's box of similar demands all over the border areas...'

'I understand, Sir.'

'Well then, Lieutenant. Let's get cracking, shall we?'

Before noon, Akash was in his new office, an unprepossessing one-roomed tenement abutting a hillside close to the Great Monastery in Tawang town. This was a good thing and a bad thing—good because it brought him closer to his target, which was the people of Tawang in whom he was now required to strike a chord through his efforts at bonding. Moreover, he rather fancied being close to the Golden Namgyal Lhatse, the Great Monastery—a repository of the Monpas' unflinching faith in the Buddha and his illustrious successor Padmasambhava.

The unpleasant feature of being cooped up in this shabby little room away from Brigade HQ was that he would be cut off from his colleagues most of the time, and instead hobnobbing with civilians. Even so early into his career, Akash harboured the serviceman's almost ingrained suspicion of civilians. Well, at least these Monpas were an inoffensive, soft-spoken people, not like the raucous, overly sensitive civilian busybodies found all over India. He knew there were many among his countrymen who thought soldiers were a necessary evil, prone to unnecessary violence, and often out of control.

But there was always the Officers' Mess to catch up with the military grapevine, he told himself. Moreover, he would continue to share quarters with Aslam, unless the Adjutant should insist that the officer in charge of Operation Sadbhavana must also live among the people of Tawang.

That might not be such a bad idea, thought the new outreach in charge. If he was to generate any measure of amity between the army in Tawang and the people of this place, he might do this better by living in their midst, learning about their lifestyle, their priorities. For the Government of India, Arunachal is a strategic asset, whereas for the natives it is home, where they have lived, multiplied and flourished for generations.

Akash was still wondering how he was going to begin his outreach and investigate the Gram Panchayat Association's claim when his orderly entered, accompanied by an elderly Monpa dressed rather like a civilian official—in a bandhgala coat and trousers, rather than the local costume or the Monpas' preferred western attire of jeans, T-shirts, etc.

'This is Mr Ralte, Saabji,' the jawan introduced the visitor to his officer. To the guest he nodded, asking him to sit down in the only chair facing Akash's official seat across his table.

'Yes, do sit down, please,' Akash extended his right hand in welcome, and the visitor took it and shook hands, warmly. Then the officer gazed at his assistant, as if to ask, 'What's going on here...who is this?'

'Mr Ralte is president of the panchayat, Saabji. And, he has organized a town hall meeting tomorrow, in the courtyard of the Great Monastery. At least two hundred citizens of Tawang will attend it, Saabji.'

Akash didn't know what to say. He knew he hadn't issued any instructions to his orderly, or anyone else, to organize a meeting with the native population. In fact, he was still mulling over his new responsibility of generating 'sadbhavana'—goodwill—for the Army in the people of Tawang. In any case, the Major had been clear, that this 'investigation' of the gram panchayats' claim for a memorial was only an exercise in circumlocution.

Since he would have time on his hands, Akash had decided to read up about the history of this region, including the 1962 conflict, where the Indian Army had suffered a rout in the then North-East Frontier Agency (NEFA) province. Tawang had been the epicentre of much of that action.

As if to help him resolve his dilemma, Mr Ralte said, 'We know you are in charge of expediting our application, Sir. Everything is ready for tomorrow's meeting...where the people of Tawang will express how strongly they feel about this matter...'

'Oh?' Akash couldn't think of much else to say, as the panchayat president stood up and extended his hands again, beaming at the Lieutenant.

The meeting in the vast—by Tawang standards—courtyard of the Great Gompa was a resounding success, if the enthusiasm of the participants was anything to go by. Everyone, it seemed, had a point of view on the 1962 war and the respective contributions of the Indian Army and the local population. After the concluding speech by no less than the Rinpoche of the monastery and Akash's brief vote of thanks to the organizers and the people of Tawang, he walked towards the monastery gates, wondering whether there was anything more substantial to the gram panchayats' claims than these emotional outpourings. If this was all there was to it, it wasn't going to be very difficult for him to put up the sort of memorandum the Adjutant proposed, closing the file on mythical Monpa heroes.

'There's one thing more, Sir,' Mr Ralte walked up to Akash, interrupting his stream of thought, and said, 'there is one person I would like you to meet...'

'Who...'

'This way...please follow me,' said the village headman, and led Akash and his assistant through a narrow lane, leading off from the gates of the great monastery. They walked for about ten minutes, until they arrived at a relatively open vista, where stood a double-storeyed house with a low door. It was one of the typical stone and bamboo Monpa dwellings that Akash had seen hereabouts, only much older and larger. There was even a small, well-kept flower bed in front of the house.

As soon as the three men entered the house, with Mr Ralte leading, an elderly woman in Monpa attire shuffled forward to greet them. To Akash's great surprise, she spoke rather good Hindi. She was very fair-complexioned, even for a Monpa, and her skin quite wrinkled. But her eyes were bright and alert, with crow's feet at the corners, suggested a sense of humour.

'Please be seated,' she couldn't have been less than eighty years old, thought Akash.

As if in reply to his curiosity, the headman whispered into Akash's ear, 'This is my wife. She's not as old as she looks, eh... only about sixty-five, Sir.'

Their host insisted that the visitors should first eat the

snacks and finish the *apang* beer, which were already waiting on a cane teapoy when they entered. The rice beer was rather rejuvenating, and the snacks, of a type Akash hadn't ever tasted before, were delicious.

When they had finished, the headman addressed his wife in Hindi so that the Lieutenant also could follow their conversation, 'Akash is investigating the events of 1962, as I told you. I did tell you about the representation we have made…'

She merely smiled, and sat with her hands folded in her lap.

'Now, I want you to tell the Lieutenant about everything that happened then. Everything! Hide nothing from him…he is an army official, as you can see, and his report will go to the government. Maybe, things will start moving now.'

The old woman continued to smile at Akash, but seemed reluctant to speak as directed by her husband, Gram Pradhan though he might be.

'You must speak,' the headman urged her, 'It is not your story alone…this concerns all the people of Tawang. It is now a part of our history, you understand?'

'I…I…it was all so long ago…' she began, hesitantly, 'And…I can hardly remember anything…' she paused, again, clearly reluctant to address the subject.

Mr Ralte touched his wife's clasped fingers gently, saying, 'Take your time…but it is important that you recall all that happened. There is no one else, you understand?'

# 3

No one imagined there would be war, least of all Sela. She was happy wandering about the hills and the forests in her red chemise with a blue sash and her yak's hair cap that sported a brightly coloured pheasant's plume. She would tease the villagers with her practical jokes, when she was not busy participating in the political discussions that preoccupied her father's cronies. After all, Sela's father was the Gam Budha—the village headman—and even the Assistant Political Officer (APO) in Tawang consulted him sometimes about the affairs of the region. Once in a while, the two men might even get to talking about the Chinese. That was when the discussions would become heated among Sela's father's acquaintances, for everyone had very strong views about the Chinese.

Some of the villagers were happy that the Indians and the Chinese were 'Bhai-Bhai', because this facilitated the villagers' movement on both sides of a loose, rather uncertain, border. They could sell milk, *churpi*, yak's meat and wool to anyone they chose, to make some extra money.

But there were those who viewed the Chinese with suspicion. 'Why must they have so many soldiers in this area if they are our brothers?' these villagers asked. 'They are building roads and bridges all over the place, as if they were preparing for some great event. The Government of India should also move its army here and do likewise—construct roads, repair bridges… At least, it will make our lives easier.'

Some even went so far as to say, 'The Delhi government must arm us villagers to tackle these Chinese… they're tricky fellows…'

But Delhi, as always, preferred talks and peaceful solutions. Prime Minister Nehru was an international statesman, respected all over the world, and he believed that India and China—two newly independent peoples—had a great future together.

One day, the village received a newspaper, several days old, with a large picture of the two great leaders Pundit Nehru and Premier Chou En-lai shaking hands, while they smiled benignly for the camera. The very next day, the villagers were astounded to see a young stranger among them, wearing a Gam Budha's red coat with a large flower stuck in a buttonhole on his chest and a white cap mounted jauntily on his head. There was a hopeful whisper among the villagers—some great leader had actually come to visit from Delhi, after all—until somebody realized that it was Sela pulling a fast one. They scolded and chased her, but naturally, the teenager was too fleet-footed to be caught.

'I was only trying to bring some cheer to this boring place, father!' Sela exclaimed when her father gently twisted her ears. 'I sense that everyone is very grim these days, like the rain clouds before they shed their water upon our valleys. Even that *sarkari babu* in the black coat and brown hat who comes to see you. He behaves as if his mother-in-law is chasing him. I decided to lighten their burden, that's all…'

'This is no laughing matter, child,' admonished Sela's father, shaking one finger and his head, knowing full well that his daughter would only think up another prank the moment she was out of sight. 'What was he going to do with this footloose tomboy?' he wondered then as he often had over the years while rearing his two motherless daughters. Noora, on the other hand, was a responsible girl. He nodded with satisfaction. Noora was reserved and sensible; she would never bring shame upon her father.

'Go and help your sister in the kitchen sometimes. She is only a year older than you are. How I wish she were several years older!' the Gam Budha sighed. 'Once my Noora is married, I can rest assured that you will be well looked after. But Noora… she ignores all my pleas, says "no" to every marriage proposal…'

'Why don't you get me married, father?' chirped Sela. 'I am ready and willing. After all, what is the difference? My husband and I will look after Noora, won't we?'

'Off with you, little imp!' and he brandished his official stick at her, sending Sela scurrying away to find someone else to torment.

Sela, in her own ingenuous way, was not far off the mark with her assessment of the situation. Storm clouds were gathering over the 'Bhai-Bhai' relationship, and there might be thunder and rain anytime soon. Rumours began to fly as fast as the scattered raindrops that chased one another over the craggy mountain peaks.

Even so, when the first Indian soldiers came marching into the Kameng Division, the villagers imagined that they would get right down to the business of laying some badly needed roads among the glens and valleys, if not the high mountain passes, and repair a few of the dilapidated bridges across the mountain torrents, which went by the inappropriate name of rivers. The villagers welcomed the men in olive green and khaki uniforms, offering them salt tea with yak's milk and yak's butter to go with the meatballs, which the soldiers relished.

But for some inexplicable reason, after the first few euphoric days, the soldiers remained in their makeshift camps and barracks, cleaning and priming their Lee-Enfield rifles and scraping rust off their bayonets.

A few days later came news that the Indians had attacked the Chinese. This was followed by rumours that the Chinese had attacked first, and killed some Indian soldiers, who were only trying to set up some posts in the mountains.

Then one day, the APO from Tawang town came to the village with a crestfallen look and told the Gam Budha that the villagers must stop crossing over to trade with the Chinese. War had officially been declared. But when she saw her father's dour countenance, Sela only quipped, 'Don't worry, father. One Indian soldier is as good as three hundred of those Chinese. This fighting will soon be over and your Noora will get married. So will I, and then, you will have many grandchildren. Do you want me to go looking for a groom for our Noora, among the Indian soldiers? I hear there are some good-looking boys in the Army camp...'

The old man was livid and shouted at his daughter, 'I forbid you to go near those soldiers, girl! This is no time for your pranks. Now, I must discuss serious affairs with the Tsopa. Go help your sister clean those goral pelts that Thabo brought, while I am busy at the village council. We need more clothing for the coming winter. Do you understand?'

Her nose wrinkled, 'That herder? Why do you let him into the house? He reeks of sheep and yak droppings...'

'Off with you!' he scolded. 'Thabo has a *broke* in the high hills, with lots of cattle. He will make a good husband for someone... someday...'

He never stopped wondering at the difference in his daughters' temperaments. They looked so like one another, although Noora was a little over a year older. In fact, it was one of Sela's pranks to go about wearing her sister's plain yak's hair cap and clothes, so that people might mistake her for the sober, sensible Noora. It was only when the packet of churpi turned out to be a lump of salt, or the can of milk transformed into plain water, that they realized Sela had put one across them.

'Enough is enough!' he exclaimed the next morning. 'Take the churpi that your sister has prepared to the market. If you come back without selling it, I will take a stick to you, girl! You are not a child anymore.'

The father was surprised, when Sela complied without protest this morning. As usual, her best friend, little Rincin, was in tow as Sela made her way to the market. And before the two girls, one seventeen and pretty and the other a toothy nine years old, could find a place to spread their wares, Rincin said conspiratorially, 'Can't we do this after a while?'

'Why...but I must sell this.' For once, Sela's conscience struggled with the urge to yield to the diversion she was sure Rincin was suggesting.

'It's a wrestling match, silly,' hissed the little girl. 'It will be over within an hour at most. Anyway...it's always that hulk Thabo who wins.'

Sela pouted, 'I don't want to go to see him.'

'Not him, silly. Who knows…maybe he will meet his match today.'

'Not today…not ever,' Sela shook her head, but let Rincin drag her toward the maidan behind the great monastery, where a crowd had already gathered to watch their heroes. Sela's free spirit hated chores, loved action, even if it was only unwashed men fighting.

As if to underline the inevitability of Rincin's prediction, the bulky yak herder had already lifted and thrown one opponent onto the spectators, by the time the two girls reached the wrestling arena and squeezed their way through the irritated crowd to reach the front row. Thabo was now strutting about on the grassy arena, roaring challenges. Then his eyes caught sight of Sela, and his shouts became louder.

'Is there a man among you?" bellowed the yak herder. 'Who is willing test me?'

'Look!' said Rincin, digging an elbow into Sela's ribs, 'look at those soldiers.'

At the same moment that Sela's eyes fell upon the trio of Indian soldiers in the front row, Thabo, as if sensing her gaze, also caught sight of the Indians. Now he marched towards them.

'You…Indians. You call yourself soldiers? Do you want to go a round with me? Or are you only brave behind your weapons?'

'Oh my god!' whispered Rincin, 'He's challenging them. What'll happen now!'

'I wish…' Sela's wish remained unspoken, for at that moment one of the three soldiers stepped into the ring.

'Listen, people of Tawang,' said the soldier in Hindi, with a smile. 'We are here to protect you from the Chinese, who are the nation's enemies. We have no wish to fight you, but…'

'Yes!' Now another of the trio also took a couple of steps

forward, 'We cannot refuse a challenge like this. It so happens that we have with us the champion of our battalion. Jaswant... Jaswant Singh Rawat will fight your champion...if you wish...'

Thabo roared and thumped his chest. The crowd cheered raucously. But the soldiers were arguing among themselves. The man called Jaswant seemed reluctant. Then a shout rang out, close at hand.

'*Darpok*!' It was a girl's voice.

At this scream, everyone looked at Sela, for it was she who had exclaimed, almost involuntarily. Slowly, his eyes locked on the young Monpa girl in the yak's hair cap with a garish plume, Jaswant stepped into the ring, unbuttoning his khaki uniform shirt.

As the crowd roared approbation, sensing a contest after all, Thabo made his move. His idea was to surprise his opponent, who was still an unknown quantity. Shrewd fighter as he was, the local hero wanted to give his adversary no opportunity to dominate.

But if Thabo had expected to surprise his opponent, he was mistaken. Jaswant sidestepped nimbly, so that the champion's rush took him stumbling past and almost into the crowd.

Thabo recovered quickly and the wrestlers circled, sizing each other up. Again Thabo lunged, and once more Jaswant skipped out of reach. But before his opponent could recover, this time he pounced and caught the herder's neck in a grip. The spectators gasped. Nobody had ever done that to Thabo before.

But the champion wasn't done, yet. With a howl of rage, he straightened up, pulling Jaswant off his feet with sheer strength. Together they fell, each trying to get a hold. Then they rose and circled, again. It was Jaswant who closed this time, trying for a grip on his adversary's thigh. But Thabo had seen it coming, and struck such a blow that Jaswant fell to the mud, all the wind knocked out of him. In a flash, the herder was upon his opponent's back, twisting his arms, inexorably.

'You shouldn't have said that,' hissed Rincin, looking scared. 'See what you've done. Thabo will kill the poor fellow. He will...'

The crowd's roars were reaching a crescendo, as they sensed their champion winning.

Jaswant writhed in the herder's powerful grasp. Thabo now had a forearm about his throat, was slowly strangling him while he used his other hand to twist the soldier's right arm to breaking point.

Sela had eyes only for the man whom she had sent, she thought, to defeat if not his death. Again, a scream escaped her lips. 'Jas...want!'

Rincin looked at her friend in bewilderment as the prostrate soldier's head twisted with a mighty, despairing effort, his eyes again meeting Sela's gaze.

It was as if a magical transformation came upon him. A sudden surge of energy shot through the dust caked, compact figure of the soldier, and his body heaved. Thabo went toppling over. As the herder stumbled, trying to regain balance, Jaswant put his head down and rushed him. An instant later, he had raised the herder's massive frame on his shoulders, and then lifted him over his head with his arms, as if he were a feather.

A groan of despair and awe rent the audience, as Thabo's body went flying through the air and landed a few yards away, bouncing a couple of times before lying still.

'This is truly a miracle,' said the girls' father, when Sela returned with empty containers and a jingling purse that afternoon, having sold all her churpi.

'We met a soldier today,' Rincin said to Noora, taking her aside so that the old man might not hear. 'Actually...three soldiers...one of them is a wrestler. He defeated Thabo...and he looked at Sela.'

'Oh?' Noora didn't quite know what to say to this. 'I've told you a dozen times to keep away from those wrestling matches. All sorts of people come there...'

'I am glad your sister is turning over a new leaf,' the father said to Noora later that night, when Sela had gone to sleep. 'Tomorrow, send her to the military camp with churpi and milk. I hear that the soldiers' kitchen is running short of supplies. They can use as much of it as we can supply. This is a great opportunity. We must not let it pass.'

'But is it a good thing to have soldiers here, father? Doesn't this mean there will be fighting?'

'No one knows...' shrugged the old man, and went off to listen to his radio, the only one in all of Tawang's Monpa homes. Although this version of Marconi's great invention produced more crackling noises than actual words, by long experience and through keeping his ears clapped to the contraption for hours on end, the old man was able to decipher the news broadcast by All India Radio or some other station, occasionally.

Later that night, Noora and Sela's father had mixed feelings, when the voice on the radio relayed the news of how Prime Minster Nehru had told Parliament resolutely—'Our Army will throw the Chinese out...like that!'

The Gam Budha was now afflicted by the eternal ambivalence of the common man, who must make both ends meet, and have peace to do so. Everyone, including him, wanted peace in Tawang, and the soldiers back where they had come from. But on the other hand, supplying provisions to the Indian military was a good opportunity for people here to make some much-needed cash.

# 4

'What's the matter with her?'

'Let me speak to her, father,' said Noora to her mystified parent. Although Noora was just about nineteen, she was as close to a mother for Sela as the girls had known, since their mother passed away many years ago. Sela would confide in her regarding matters she was scared to discuss with her father.

But Noora soon realized that her sibling was in dead earnest about not carrying the churpi and milk to the military camp. When pressed, all Sela had to say was, 'I know the burden is too much upon you, sister. Besides, if father wants me to help you, I have to stay home and learn to do all the chores. How else am I going to learn?'

'Is this you talking, you little ragamuffin?' demanded Noora, playfully tapping her sister's head.

'Think what you want,' said Sela, 'But I am not going to meet those soldiers again. They scare me.'

'Hmm…' was all that Noora said.

When she broached the subject with Rincin, the little girl had this to say, 'I don't blame your sister for being afraid, Noora. You know, you should have seen the way that soldier looked at

Sela. I was certain he was coming for us, after he thrashed Thabo. He might have killed us…that is why we fled, don't you see?'

Noora wondered. Realizing there was no point arguing any further, she decided to take on the responsibility of carrying the provisions to sell to the military kitchen. Slowly, she trudged the mile or so to the undulating meadow where the Indians were bivouacked, with the sacks of churpi and meat slung from straps on her back and a can of milk in either hand.

She was sweating by the time she arrived at the camp, and made her way to a large tent towards which she had been directed by the sentries. This was the kitchen. She was wondering whether she should set down her burden, and look for someone to speak to, when a soldier in khaki half trousers and a woollen sweater sauntered up. Without a word he came up to her and helped her lower the heavy sacks to the ground.

Relieved of the weight, she whipped off her cap and wiped the sweat off her brows. Her cheeks were even ruddier than usual, thanks to the warm sun and exertion.

'What is it you have there?' he asked nonchalantly in Hindi, the universal language of the Indian Military.

'Oh, thank you,' she replied instinctively in Monpa dialect, and then in broken Hindi, 'Thank you, Saabji.'

She looked at the young, bright face, with a clipped moustache above the lips that smiled easily. Suddenly, she felt embarrassed by his steady, frank gaze.

'No, not Saabji…I'm just a soldier,' he chuckled, pointing to the sacks, and repeated his question, 'What are you carrying in there?' which reminded her of the purpose of her visit.

She hastened to unpack, and broke off a piece of churpi, handing it to him. He took it without any hesitation, and munched on the cheese.

'Mm...that's delicious,' he nodded, 'Almost as good as my mother prepares.'

Although she couldn't understand everything he said, it was obvious he liked the churpi.

'What is your name?' he asked. That was a question she understood.

'Noora,' she said, apprehensively.

'Noora,' he repeated, and the accompanying smile seemed to imply that he approved.

Always shy and withdrawn even among her own people, she was now becoming distinctly uncomfortable at being alone with this stranger. She wished she could hand over these sacks to whoever had the authority, take the money and leave.

'There you are!' the shout interrupted Noora's reverie, probably saving her from further embarrassment. The speaker was another soldier, also in shorts but with only a vest covering his bulky torso. He was one of a group of three, the other two wearing woolen sweaters like the soldier she had been conversing with. As the newcomers came alongside, she did notice that her acquaintance was taller and better looking than his colleagues.

Almost as soon as the thought occurred, she chided herself. What are you thinking? You're here to do a job. Better do it and get going. These men are Indian soldiers.

'So? What are you doing here?' Trilok clapped Jaswant on his shoulder. 'Were you trying to keep the girl all to yourself?

'I think our friend is more interested in those,' chuckled Gopal, pointing to the sacks. 'He's always the first to arrive when there's food to be had, eh...heh...'

Trilok turned to the man in the vest, who had already taken charge of Noora's merchandise, 'Better carry that stuff into your kitchen, Ramratan, before this glutton gets his hands on any more of it.'

Jaswant and his friends laughed, while the cook lugged the sacks into the tent. The three friends continued their banter, glancing intermittently at Noora. She stood fidgeting, embarrassed by all the attention.

Her discomfort increased so much that she half turned and began to move slowly away, as if with the intention of leaving the spot, when the cook emerged from the kitchen, calling, 'Hey, wait! Don't you want your cash and milk cans?'

Hurrying back, she snatched the welcome currency and the empty cans from the cook's fingers. Quickly tucking the money into her purse, she made haste to leave the vicinity of the military camp.

By and by, Noora got over her excitement, her steps slowing for once as she neared home, as if she wished to linger on her thoughts. Try as she might to preoccupy herself with other things, including the happiness it would bring her father to know the Indian soldiers had so readily accepted their churpi, meat and milk, her thoughts kept returning to the tall, young soldier with a moustache. Then, she recalled with surprise that she had forgotten even to get his name, although she told him her own.

But the atmosphere at home was fraught, when Noora returned from her errand.

The cause of anxiety was a visitor. The yak herder Thabo was in a foul temper. He did not care if the girls' father was the Gam Budha, he was almost shouting. After all, he was somebody, too. In fact, he was a person of considerable means, the yak herder seemed at pains to assert—which was a fact, Noora knew, considering he owned a broke, a yak ranch in the high mountains.

'I am willing to offer five yaks for your daughter,' he was growling, when Noora entered the house. He glanced briefly at her, while her father cast a hopeful, despairing look in her direction.

'No, no. It is not this one I am talking about,' said Thabo, 'I want the other one, your younger daughter…as I have been saying all these months.'

The knowledge that the yak herder didn't want her only made Noora hate him more, although she tried to quell the emotion. She was always trying to convince herself that it was only natural that Sela should have more suitors, since she was far more attractive. If a proposal had come for Sela, so be it. In any case, she was not going to leave her father alone, at this stage in his life.

But the father was firm on this count. 'I know I have to marry off both my daughters, Thabo. But Noora is older…if only you were to agree…'

'I will wait until you can find a match for her,' Noora heard the visitor say, while she got busy preparing a snack for the two men, to go with the inevitable rice beer. 'But I must have your younger daughter. That was the deal, and I will not change my mind. Five yaks are what I am offering. There are households that will offer me two daughters for that many heads of cattle…'

Thabo glanced towards the bamboo partition screening the kitchen where Noora was busy, but the old man shook his head, 'Although custom permits, that is not something I can do. I do not believe a man should have two wives at the same time.'

'Suit yourself, old man. But I will not wait indefinitely. And I cannot stand for my betrothed…er…your daughter… humiliating me before other men…Indian soldiers at that. I do not wish to drag you before the village council, but if my hand is forced…'

'Let me speak to my daughter, Thabo. In fact, it seems that she has become a new person. She has been working at home all day yesterday and this morning. She has even gone to the market to sell churpi, today. Maybe she will see reason.'

'She had better…as I said, if it hadn't been for her distracting me, I would not have lost the wrestling bout to that blasted Indian.' Thabo's angry gaze rested on Noora, as she entered with the beer and snacks. 'Why don't you train that girl to be responsible like this one, old man?'

The host said nothing, pretending to be absorbed in the flavour of the beer.

'I'll be going now,' said the yak herder, getting to his feet as soon as he had finished the food and drink, 'I hope to see a different, sensible girl two days from now at the festival. That will be as good an occasion as any for us to get engaged.'

Sela's father nodded, exchanging an anxious glance with Noora, who stood with eyes downcast and fingers intertwined over the folds of her long skirt.

In fact, Sela might not have attended the Lhabab Duchen celebrations that year at all, if her friend Rincin hadn't threatened that their friendship would be at an end, if she didn't participate in the pantomime. The cronies always donned one of the lion or the peacock masks together at the festival dance, and this year was going to be no exception—Rincin swore with tears in her eyes.

'Besides,' said the little girl, 'What are you sacred of? The Indians won't come to our festival, I bet. They are too busy preparing to drive the Chinese away from the borders of our country. My father says there is already fighting going on somewhere and all these soldiers will go there sooner rather than later.'

'Don't say that. If there is fighting, men will die.'

'But isn't that what soldiers are meant for...to die?' asked Rincin, naively, as the two girls in their colourful best tripped over grass, rock and bramble to reach the venue.

Rincin's father's clairvoyance seemed justified, when the girls joined the throng at the large ground near the monastery, where the celebrations were taking place. People from all eight villages scattered about the fertile pastures of Tawang crowded the area, and most of them were talking about the gathering war clouds.

Commemorating as it does the descent of Gautama Buddha from Tushita, the abode of the Lord, the festivities this year seemed touched by a rare poignancy, with the threat of violence looming over these usually sleepy mountains and valleys. But while the comings and goings of political functionaries and the movement of military men and vehicles hinted at the presence of an enemy at the gates, there was still no imminent danger, was the general consensus, and therefore, no reason to call off or even tone down the celebrations.

Although Noora accompanied her sister and Rincin only reluctantly, once they reached the scene of festivities, the colour and vibrancy of so many happy faces affected even her normally reticent spirit.

Her blood positively raced, when she caught a glimpse of khaki uniforms amid the maroon, yellow and white of the people's festive dresses and the flags festooning the vicinity. An instinctive glance told her that Sela and Rincin had long abandoned her to her solitary ways, and merged with the raucous crowd. That was a relief. She was afraid one of them might have caught her looking in the direction of the trio of soldiers. Although she tried not to look, her eyes were drawn again and again to the men.

He was there, of course, and his two friends.

'Where is your sister?' Thabo's query jolted her back to reality.

'Oh…ah…' she stuttered, hoping the man hadn't noticed the soldiers, or her covert glances.

'She must dance with me today wearing one of those masks. That is the custom,' continued Thabo, frowning. Even the yak herder was dressed in his best clothes, having shed his customary herder's outfit that reeked of sweat and animal droppings.

'Ah, yes…yes. Of course. She…Sela was here a moment ago. She…she must be somewhere in that crowd, naturally. You know how my sister likes to mix with anyone and everyone.' Knowing her sister's aversion to the man, she tried to postpone the inevitable by saying, on an impulse, 'I…I will dance with you, until we find her.'

Thabo agreed reluctantly, and they moved towards the dancing crowd, holding hands, Noora praying fervently all the while that none of the soldiers should notice her presence. If that happened, they might hail her, which could only lead to more acrimony between Thabo and the soldiers. For some inexplicable reason, she felt protective towards the soldiers.

Noora and Thabo joined the crowd of dancers, with Thabo still shooting hopeful looks in all directions for a glimpse of Sela.

That was unlikely, since at that very moment Noora's sibling and Rincin were inside one of the prancing, twisting lion masks with a long tail. In fact, the little girl was saying to her friend,

'I have to go and take a pee...do you mind? I cannot hold it any longer. You just keep jumping as if there are two of us in here, so that no one else takes my place. Understand?'

But as Rincin was racing off to find a secure hedge behind which to do her business, she also noticed the three soldiers strolling about, watching the crowd. On an impulse, the little girl changed direction and approached the Indians. She would ask them why they were not away fighting, instead of wasting their time here.

'Hey, isn't that the companion of the girl who called our friend a coward?' asked Gopal, as soon as he saw Rincin approaching.

'Yes, and I think she has something to say to us,' nodded Trilok, winking at Jaswant, 'You want to find out where she's hiding, Jaswant...your heart-throb?'

'I barely know her,' was the reply.

'So why have you been trying to learn the Monpa's language from the porters at the camp...huh?'

Jaswant shrugged, 'I thought I might as well...there is no knowing how much time we might have to spend here, see?'

'Is that also why you were trying to make friends with her sister, the other day?'

'I was only being civil to a hardworking young woman, fellows...'

But their conversation was interrupted as Rincin marched up to say, 'Are you here looking for my friend Sela, darpok?'

Jaswant was taken aback at the Hindi epithet for coward, but his friends laughed uproariously.

'What if I were?' he asked warily, speaking to her in broken Monpa and deciding there was no point in taking umbrage at the child's prattle. 'Sela? Do you know where she is?'

'Who else would know, solider? I am her best friend, all right?' she turned and pointed, 'You see that lion mask dancing… over there?'

'You mean…'

'Yes…but I must be going. I can't hold it any longer…' and Rincin raced away.

Before his friends could quite figure out his intentions, Jaswant had marched off in the direction the child indicated. Trilok and Gopal saw him lift the mask and disappear inside it, and turned to one another with knowing smiles.

If Sela was flabbergasted when the person entering the lion face turned out to be a man instead of Rincin, Jaswant was equally overwhelmed to set eyes on her again, for the second time. He had never seen a more beautiful girl in all his life! They stared at one another for a long minute, stupefied. Then he said, gently, stabbing at his own chest with one forefinger to make his meaning clear, 'Coward? Do you still think I am a coward?'

She blushed, and the sudden rush of blood to her cheeks only made her more attractive. He wanted to gather her in his arms at that moment. But he couldn't do that, of course. He barely knew her.

'If you dance with me inside this mask I will know you are not,' was her reply.

From her gestures, he understood what she meant. 'What… what about your little friend?'

'Oh…Rincin? She will understand,' said Sela. 'She is my best friend. Besides, she has lots of friends in this crowd, and she will not miss my presence for a while.'

When Rincin did return to look for the lion mask with her best friend inside, more than half an hour later, both were missing. She wondered for a moment whether the soldiers had taken her friend away. But then, she decided that was unlikely, considering how scared Sela was of the soldiers.

By and by, she ran into Noora, who was also looking for Sela. 'I think that big yak herder must have found her after all,' said Rincin. She made a face, 'You must try and stop him from marrying your sister. If that happens, I will have no one left to spend time with.'

'Ah…don't you worry on that account. You can always come home and help with the chores,' Noora patted the child's head, 'I will teach you to dry meat and make churpi. That way, your parents will be proud of you.'

'No,' said Rincin, with a resolute shake of her head, 'I do not want to make churpi. I have decided that I am going to be a soldier when I grow up. By the way, do you know they were here today?'

'Who?' asked Noora, tremulously, as if she knew what was coming.

'Those three soldiers, including the one who thrashed Thabo and chased us…' As she spoke, Rincin felt a twinge of guilt that she had revealed Sela's whereabouts to the soldier. What if he had taken Sela away and killed her in revenge for calling him a coward? So she decided to speak no more of it, and said instead, 'Can we go home, Noora? I am tired and sleepy.'

For her part, Noora was relieved to get away from there. Nor did she wish to reveal the fact that she also had seen them, including the soldier with the moustache who made her heart beat faster.

# 5

The moment she saw the cast of her father's features, Noora realized that something was seriously amiss. It was as if the dark cumulus of conflict enveloping their hard but placid lives was finding its reflection upon the visage of this Gam Budha, literally old man of the village, who was responsible for safeguarding the welfare of his people and their ways.

Was the enemy creeping up on Tawang? Would the soldiers leave soon to join the fighting, she caught herself wondering. Still, she was not unduly worried, because, as the Khempo at the great monastery never tired of telling her, everything happens for a purpose.

Even when her father sat down upon his cot without depositing his walking stick at its appointed corner as he always did, she thought nothing of it. The sturdy, metre-long bamboo staff with a brass head was at once a symbol of his authority and a support for his ageing frame, and he treated it with great reverence. 'Maybe he was more exhausted than usual, after the festivities and the official business, all of which he had to be a part of, considering his position. A jug of rice beer would soon revive his spirits,' Noora thought, and set about preparing some food also to go with the energy drink.

When at first she heard the squeals and recognized Sela's voice, she was relieved her sister had returned, and glad to hear her excited tones. It was only when the sounds began to sound like screams, tinged with agony, that Noora became worried. Quickly pouring the beer into a jug she picked up the tray of food and hurried out, only to see a rare sight.

Despite all her pranks and at times exasperating insolence, Noora could not remember her father having ever raised a hand against his younger child. As the elder sister, Noora would occasionally be at the receiving end of a slap or a mild caning when the children got out of hand. After all, it was her job to set a good example. But Sela, he never touched.

The scene that now met her quite froze Noora in her tracks. She almost dropped the tray. Sela's sounds were now transformed into agonized howls. And no wonder. Holding her dishevelled hair in a vice-like grip with one hand, the old man was wielding his walking stick with the other. 'Thwack! Whack! Thwack!' He belaboured her mercilessly, relentlessly.

'Aiii....ooo...no...aiii,' Sela jumped and twisted, while he rained blows on her back and limbs. But he would not let go. 'Fa...father...it hurts...aiii....aiii...'

Thinking quickly, Noora slammed the tray back on her kitchen floor and rushed outside to grab her father's arms. They struggled briefly, as he continued his assault on his younger progeny, but eventually Noora put in all her strength and managed to hold his arms, so that Sela could escape his grip.

'Go...get out of here...quickly!' Noora told her. Instead of leaving the scene, Sela rushed off into a corner of the house and threw herself upon a couch, her body wracked by sobs.

'What were you hitting her like that for?' Noora asked her father, forcing him gently but firmly into his chair. 'Have we become a burden that you want to kill your daughter? If you are angry about something, kill me instead. But lay not a finger on my sister...'

The old man sat in his chair looking dazed and lost, as if he had no words to answer his daughter's accusations. Moved by his melancholy, Noora sat down at his feet and clasped his hands. Caressing the gnarled fingers, she said softly, 'Maybe she has done wrong, father. But does the Sakya Muni not say that forgiveness is a great virtue...that violence achieves nothing? You must stop worrying, father...'

He did not reply, continuing to stare with a frozen gaze out into the verdant, rocky landscape of this land, which had nurtured his ancestors for generations but was now under threat from an immeasurable enemy—war. Yet, the war without was as nothing compared to the conflict that raged within the father's choking heart. Noora realized that he had hurt himself more by his violence than the child he vented his frustrations upon.

She also knew he would say no more on the subject, and so she did not press the matter. She gave him food and waited by his side until he lay down to sleep. Then, she stole across to where Sela was still hunched upon her cot, with no more tears to shed. Gently, Noora cajoled her little sister into eating some food, then took her head in her lap and sang a lullaby to the seventeen-year old, as if she were a baby.

She guessed what might have happened. Her father's rage was no doubt prompted by another complaint from Thabo, and probably even an appeal by the yak herder to the village elders. Nothing could be more humiliating for her father, she knew, than to have his integrity questioned.

She wondered whether Sela had spent her time during the

Lhubab Duchen celebrations with the young soldier she claimed to be afraid of. Considering her own ambiguous feelings for that Indian with the moustache who liked to eat her churpi, Noora could understand Sela's state of mind. Was her sibling in love? Was she herself also in love? Was this, indeed, love? Would the sisters' affections ever be requited?

Despite lying awake almost half the night while her father and sister slept the sleep of the dead, exhausted no doubt by their emotions, Noora as always was the first to rise. The sun was already dappling pastures around the village, when she went out of doors to breathe and reassure herself that it was not yet the end of the world. A shoot of cautious hope began to sprout within her. The best way to keep this sapling alive, she realized, was to get down to her chores. It is work, the drudgery of everyday existence, the minutes and hours of effort that leads to a better, brighter tomorrow.

Such were her thoughts, as she first neatly packed dried meat and churpi in sacks, poured milk into two cans and went looking for Rincin. Fortunately, the little girl was awake. 'Come over and help me with the sacks, girl,' she said to the child. When she was all loaded with the provisions and ready to leave, she told Rincin, 'Now you stay back here and make sure Sela comes to no harm. The old man is asleep, too. Look after them, while I deliver this stuff to the military camp. Can you do this much without getting up to any more mischief?'

'You can trust me,' murmured the child, looking contrite. She appeared to have guessed what might have happened at Noora's house. 'It wasn't my fault anyway that your sister ran off with the soldier yesterday at the festival. I thought she was afraid of him...that they hated one another. How was I to know they would spend so many hours together?'

'What's done is done,' said Noora, sternly. 'Speak no more of it.'

Meanwhile, Jaswant was mulling over the cook Ramratan's advice. 'What's done cannot be undone, my young friend. It's not your fault that you fell for a Monpa beauty. The heart answers to no one but itself. No one knows better than me... I have had two lovers and two wives...'

'Oh, is that so?' wondered Jaswant, 'How can you be in love with two people at the same time?'

'You got it wrong,' said the cook, swatting his colleague's hand away as Jaswant reached for a piece of the potatoes he was peeling to prepare puri bhaji for the company's breakfast. 'And I don't mean the potatoes...love. I agree it happens only once in a lifetime. But in my case, my first love died soon after we married. Then I met her cousin and fell in love with her... you see? She is now my wife...so, technically, it is possible to love two women at the same time...'

'But your first wife passed on, you said...'

'Fool! I haven't stopped loving her, for that reason.' Ramratan dropped handfuls of the boiled, peeled potatoes into the large brass vessel where they jumped and sizzled. 'Now...this girl of yours... She is a Monpa porter, right?'

'No...I don't think she's a porter...'

'Fool, they're all porters, as far as the Indian Army is concerned. My point is...she is a Monpa Buddhist and you are a Hindu Garhwali...'

'Isn't that a good thing?' demanded Trilok, chuckling as he ambled over and joined the conversation. 'They will be a happy couple...always.'

'What do you know of happiness?' demanded the cook.

'Everything,' retorted Trilok, superciliously. 'Don't you see? Jaswant and his…what's her name, eh?'

'Sela,' said Jaswant, hesitantly, 'I think her name is Sela.'

'Now, this Sela and our Jaswant will lead a blissful life, because they will not understand what they are telling one another at all, don't you see? A Monpa speaking Monpa and the other, a Garhwali—total incomprehension… That is what I call a happy marriage.'

Ramratan guffawed, and Jaswant couldn't help smiling, either. But then, his attention was distracted by the arrival of a visitor, at the periphery of the camp kitchen.

'It's that girl!' exclaimed Trilok.

'Jaswant's sweetheart?'

'No, no,' said Trilok to the cook, as Jaswant hurried off to welcome Noora. 'The one who brought the provisions, the other day. I think she is her sister. They bear a striking resemblance.'

'Do you think he is in love with both of them…that is possible, you know.' The cook had a beatific look on his face, as if he were thinking of his own two loves.

'Ah, you should concentrate on preparing food fit for human beings, Ramratan, instead of corrupting young soldiers,' Trilok playfully punched the cook's brawny shoulders.

'Get off with you,' replied the latter, 'let me take charge of those sacks before our wrestling champion gets his hands on that stuff and the rest of the company starves.'

As Ramratan made haste to claim his stock-in-trade, Jaswant walked with Noora, a short distance beyond the kitchen where they could chat undisturbed.

Although she followed him meekly, her heart was pounding. Perhaps it was a good thing that they were not familiar with one another's language, because the natural gaps in comprehension and reaction helped to veil her discomfiture.

Yet, despite her reticence, she was drawn inexorably to him. She remembered that she still did not know his name. Before she could think of a way to broach the subject, he smiled at her and said in broken Monpa dialect, 'How is your father... your sister?'

She did not recall having mentioned a sister to him. Or maybe she had. She nodded vigorously to signify that they were both well, although with a twinge of remorse that Sela was actually in not so happy a frame of mind as she might have wished...or her father, for that matter. She wished she could tell this young man that one from his own community was responsible for her sister and father's misery.

He chattered on, with an easy familiarity that was both winning and soothing. For some inexplicable reason, she found herself wanting to confide in this Indian soldier who had arrived from thousands of miles away, and whom she had known for only a few days.

Then she realized that he was saying something about his home. It seemed his family also lived in the mountains, but far away. She heard him mention the name 'Leelavati' several times. She understood from his words and gestures that he was referring to his mother. Why did she feel relieved that Leelavati was his mother? Did she fear it might have been a wife? What was that to her, in any case?

As she became familiar with his halting Monpa words, mixed with his own native tongue, she also gathered that he liked the churpi she supplied.

'Like what my mother makes,' he was saying.

She blushed. Was he paying her a compliment? Glancing

covertly at him, she realized he was gazing off into the distance, as if he were waiting for someone to appear on the horizon.

Then she thought of her sister, and was sorry for her sibling. It was unlikely that their father would let Sela out of the house for the next few days. 'Thabo was to blame,' thought Noora, and she hated him for it, although reason told her the yak herder was quite justified in his stand. He had a reputation to think of, and there was every possibility he might have taken Sela to be his wife, if that Indian soldier had not intruded and deluded Sela, whom Thabo considered his betrothed for all practical purposes.

She wondered. Might Sela's soldier also be watching the horizon at that very moment, waiting for the pretty adolescent to come bounding over a pasture like a red butterfly in a tasselled cap?

But now her musings were interrupted by Jaswant's words. He was saying something about marriage. The look in his eyes as he dwelt on the subject made her go weak in the legs. To hide her confusion she pointed to the camp kitchen, saying, 'Has your cook kept the money ready for me, I wonder...'

In fact, at that very moment they heard Ramratan's stentorian voice calling out. 'Come and get your payment, lady. I have work to do...a hundred hungry soldiers to feed.'

'Did you propose to her...I mean regarding her sister...' asked the cook, after Noora left with her money and paraphernalia.

'I...I didn't know what...how to say it...' for once, Jaswant was at a loss for words.

'Fool! Delay can be fatal...in matters of the heart...and in war. You should've told her you wished to marry her sister. That's all there is to it.'

'I did mention marriage,' squirmed Jaswant, 'But she had a

strange expression on her face...and I was afraid I might offend her...'

'Quite right, too,' agreed Trilok. 'It is best to ask the girl directly. Besides, we have a war to fight, fellows. Who is to say how many of us will return to our mothers, sisters and wives when this battle is over?'

'You are a cheerful son of a b#*$h, aren't you?' scowled the cook. 'In any case, I do have to feed the lot of you gluttons until the Chinese kill you, eh? Off with the two of you, now, if you want breakfast on time. I don't have all day, understand. And...Jaswant...'

'What?'

'If you won't speak to the lady...or her sister who you actually have the hots for...the next time this girl comes up here, I am going to make a proposal of marriage on your behalf. I cannot bear this suspense any longer.'

'Yes, yes,' chuckled Trilok, 'It's worse than waiting for the Chinese. Moreover, it is the responsibility of elders to discuss matters regarding marriage...isn't that how we do it back home?'

# 6

On her way home from the military camp, and afterwards as she went about her chores, Noora could not shake off the effects of her encounter with her soldier that morning. 'Her' soldier? When he spoke of his home and mother, and praised Noora's skills as a cook, was that an oblique way of showing his interest in her? 'You are being presumptuous,' she told herself.

For once, she wished Sela would chatter incessantly about everything under the sun. But her sister was strangely subdued today. She even assisted Noora in slicing the yak's meat into thin strips and laying it out in the sun to dry. So much so that she insisted on preparing lunch, rather than leaving all activities in the kitchen to her older sister as usual.

Try as she might to discuss with Sela her conversation with the soldier that morning, Noora's courage failed. She also felt awkward that she should be presuming to raise such a matter, when the poor girl had received a thrashing on mere suspicion of associating with an Indian soldier. By the same token, I must receive a beating, too, was her guilty admission.

She had half a mind to confess as much to her father. But the old man did not return for lunch that afternoon. Instead,

Rincin poked her head through a window and called, 'Where are you, Noora and Sela? What are you doing at home when such important events are taking place in Tawang?"

'What are you talking about?' Noora let the child into the house and made her sit down with them to eat the meal.

'I am talking about the important meeting, which is taking place in the town,' said Rincin, gesticulating. 'My father came home all worked up...he said many important people from far way...a place called Dilli...have come to decide about the war. There is going to be a lot of fighting and many people will die. We may have to leave Tawang, too...'

'Now you're joking...there is no end to your exaggeration!' Sela spoke up now, her spirits reviving under the salve of her best friend's enthusiasm. 'How can we leave Tawang? This is where we live.'

'Sela is right for once,' nodded Noora, 'Nothing of the kind will happen, little girl. That may be why the important people have come here, so far from their offices...to make peace with the Chinese...so that there will be no bloodshed.'

But, though she said this, Noora's heart was not so confident. Rincin's father was one of the few educated Monpas, and he was a clerk at the office of the Indian Political Officer of Tawang. He was unlikely to be spreading baseless rumours.

This news was also probably the reason for their father not coming home to eat lunch that afternoon. The Gam Budha made it a point never to miss his afternoon meal at home, unless some very pressing matters kept him away.

Still, she tried to keep the atmosphere from becoming too depressing, what with the recent violence in her own home, by telling the girls, 'The Khempo says... men should not be fighting each other, like beasts. It is only love that will preserve our world…'

At this, Rincin looked askance at her best friend, and said, 'Is that why you were with that soldier yesterday, Sela? Trying to save our world?'

'I wasn't trying to save anyone,' murmured Sela, 'I was only…okay, I'll say it. I like being with him. Is that a sin? He makes me laugh…and when I look at him, I think…soldiers cannot be bad. Not all of them.'

Alarmed as she was by her sister's brash admission, Noora was on the point of scolding her, urging her to be more circumspect, but the words she fashioned seemed unwilling to leave her lips.

Meanwhile, Rincin was saying, gravely, 'Your yak herder suitor may not agree with you. I am sure he has not forgotten the beating he got that day.'

'There's no need to bring up that incident,' chided Noora, 'Do you understand? Thabo is a person of considerable influence…'

'Then maybe I will marry him, if neither of you sisters wants to get your hands on his house and his yaks.'

'You might end up getting a spanking for your pains,' scolded Sela. 'Now run along home, and let us sisters prepare churpi and meat to sell at the military camp. There is so much work to be done…and we are going to be busy all day. You can return in the morning if you want to be of any help.'

Rincin stood up, 'Is that you speaking, Sela? Traitor!' And she marched towards the door, only to stop there for a moment to say, 'That soldier will be the death of you, stupid girl!'

As the urchin scampered away, Noora glanced quickly at her sister. But Sela wasn't paying attention, busying herself with cleaning up after their meal.

Noora shut the door and joined Sela, who said, 'I am not

going to die. I will live, even if it means selling meat and milk and churpi to the Chinese…'

When Noora did not answer, her sister continued, 'What do you think would happen, sister, if one of us were to marry someone who is from a village, thousands of miles away? Do you think we could be happy?'

Noora was quite taken aback at this question, for it echoed exactly her thoughts at that moment. To cover up her confusion, she replied, 'Right meditation is the only way to happiness, the Khempo says…'

'Tch tch! You and your Khempo!' Sela shook her head, 'What is this talk of meditation, sister? Have you never wanted to feel what it is like to be with a man? Isn't that also happiness?'

Her sister concentrated on scouring soot from the insides of a bamboo vessel.

'I am happy here, mother, although we might go to war at any moment. Also, I met a very pretty girl. I can barely have a conversation with her because we speak different languages, though I am trying to learn the Monpa tongue. Still, I like being with her…and I think she likes me, too. And, one more thing… For the first time in my life, I have tasted paneer that is almost as delicious as the stuff you make at home. Here, they call it churpi…'

At that moment, Trilok Singh Negi entered the bamboo shack, which was their quarters and said, 'Better wind up your letter, Jaswant. We're moving.'

'Says who?'

'The news is from Div HQ. There's been trouble on the Thag La ridge. Our lines there may not stand firm. The Chinese hold all the aces, is what the grapevine says.'

'Aren't the Gorkhas and Rajputs out there, near the Namka Chu? Each one of them is equal to a dozen Chinese, I tell you.'

'This is no time for bravado, Jaswant. These mountains are a different proposition. I hear that our men out there don't even have adequate rations and ammunition. If the Chinese attack...'

'So? That's good news! Maybe we can have a go at those sons of Chou En-Lai, after all.'

'Maybe...' Trilok watched his intrepid friend fold the inland letter he had been writing on. Getting to his feet, Jaswant put the blue-tinted post office stationery into a pocket of his uniform shirt that hung from a peg. Trilok continued, 'By the way, why don't you post that letter? I think you've been writing this epistle since we were in Nagaland...'

'What can I do?' smiled Jaswant, wryly. 'When we were in Ramgarh, I thought we'd be home soon in Dehradun, and I'd hand it over to my mother, instead of posting it. Because every time I am about to seal and drop it into the post bag, something interesting happens, and I decide to add that bit, too. You know how mothers are...they must know everything that has to do with their sons. And I don't want to leave anything out.'

'You do love your mother very much, don't you?'

Jaswant's eyes gleamed, 'She was the one who always believed in me, and kept me going. When the Navy sent me home for being a couple of centimetres shorter than their standard height I might have given up, but she wouldn't. She knew I had it in me to become a soldier. Someday, I want to become a Captain and live with my mother and my family in a large, comfortable house in Dehradun.'

'Not like the military farm stables, eh? I know how you feel.' Then Trilok chuckled, 'But at this rate, that letter of yours will soon resemble an old Ramayan, preserved and found by somebody else after a thousand years. Don't forget that we might be going to war, soon. There's no saying...'

'Say it, Trilok. Say it! We will all die, is that what you mean?'

The other shrugged, 'Or we might all live. *Jai Badri Vishaal*!'

'*Jai Badri Vishaal*!' came the echo as another soldier entered the shack. Gopal Gusain was already in full kit. 'We've got to fall in, quickly. There's going to be an inspection. Some senior officer is visiting, I hear.'

It was only a few days ago, it seemed, that the battalion had arrived in Tawang, after the long journey from Ramgarh. The road trip from Chariduar, in Assam, via Bhalukpong and Bomdila had been arduous, taking all of seven days. Upon arrival on the 7th of October, some of the soldiers were deployed for chopping and dragging down logs of wood from the dense forests clothing the mountains around Tawang. They were told to set up their own, makeshift quarters. The army and Assam Rifles barracks were not enough to accommodate all the new battalions trooping into NEFA. It was taxing work.

But an air of elation infected the exhausted battalion when, a couple of days after their arrival, the new Corps Commander visited Tawang and addressed the troops. They were told the victory would be quick and decisive. Some of them at least would be able to go home for Diwali. Even better, the government had decided to release some long overdue allowances for their warriors on the nation's borders.

After all, went the official line, right was on the Indian side. Nehru was an eloquent statesman of the world, while his Chinese counterpart Chou En-lai, if anything, was a double crossing so and so. The Indians would thrash the enemy in no time, and our soldiers will be able to spend their hard-earned cash at home.

The Chinese might be better armed, and in greater numbers, but they were…well, only Chinese. The Indian soldier was any day a better fighter. If they could deal with the fierce Pathans and the head hunting Nagas, the battle-hardened Indian Army was going to make short work of the Chinese hordes. Rajputs and Sikhs, Gurkhas or Garhwalis, Marathas and Jats, there was no end to the tales of valour studding the long, glorious traditions of these regiments.

But now, more than a week later, 4 Garhwal were still in the cold, inclement, drafty barracks and log huts of Tawang. Dussehra came and went, without any kind of celebration.

'You did have fun at that Monpa dance at the monastery, didn't you?' Gopal teased his friend. 'We're better off than the Rajputs and Gorkhas…'

Jaswant almost felt guilty at the thought, and his shoulders slumped. He recalled how he had been gallivanting about the green pastures scattered through Tawang, while their less fortunate colleagues faced the enemy at the Thag La ridge.

Gopal put an arm about his friend's shoulders, 'It's nobody's fault that we are all stuck here, at this time of year. I heard those poor Gorkhas were on the point of embarking for home, when the orders came for them to redeploy to the Namka Chu area.'

It was all so ironic, laughable. But nobody had the heart to, with the Punjabis and Gorkhas and Rajputs shivering and starving on the slopes south of the Namka Chu, while the slavering Chinese looked down upon them. Literally.

Worse was to come. That evening, news spread quickly through Brigade HQ and the battalion that the Corps Commander had fallen ill. General Kaul was already on his way to Delhi, to be hospitalized there. The high altitude demanded acclimatization, and even the senior staff officers were not immune to pulmonary oedema.

'What kind of a General is he?' asked Jaswant of his friends, when they returned to their bunks after a long day's military drills and other chores.

'You should hold your tongue,' said Gopal. 'You will get us all into trouble, one day. A General is a General. They have their reasons for doing the things they do.'

'We grew up hearing tales of Rana Pratap,' Jaswant was adamant. 'I would be willing to die a hundred times, if I had a leader like that...'

'And your mother...what happens to her...to our families if we die?'

'They will understand. We are soldiers. All that we need is a cause to die for.'

'You're crazy, Jaswant. It is good to be afraid, sometimes. Fear makes a person cautious, circumspect.'

'Who said I am not afraid, Gopal? But...a General...'

'Forget the General...what are you going to do about that girlfriend of yours?' Trilok asked, suddenly, blowing smoke rings before handing his cigarette to Gopal to let him light another. Jaswant was a fitness freak and kept away from cigarettes. 'She is a Monpa, isn't she? I say...if it comes to that...who will these Monpas side with—us...or the Chinese?'

Jaswant only gazed quietly back at his friends, as if his thoughts were still far away, beyond the mist of centuries, listening to the pounding hooves of Chetak, the matchless horse carrying his master to safety, after the Maharana had staked and lost all but his honour in the limestone valleys of Haldighati.

# 7

The girls' father left home early the following morning. There was a meeting of senior government officials, the Gam Budhas of the eight villages in Tawang, and some military officers.

'I will not be home for lunch today either,' said the old man. Then he called Noora aside and whispered to her, 'If you can, tell your sister that I am sorry I lost my temper. But it is only because I am conscious of our prestige among the people of Tawang. I want both of you girls to marry well, and be happy in your families after I am gone from this world. Otherwise, my spirit will linger in these mountains…and I do not want that. I seek nirvana. For that, I must perform my duties as a father as well as I can. Do you understand?'

Her father's brief speech brought tears to Noora's eyes. She hugged him and sent him on his way, with his lunch packed in a couple of containers.

'I know father was talking to you about me,' Sela sidled up to her, even as the older sister debated about how she was going to convey her father's apology to her sibling. 'It is my fault father is unhappy…isn't that so?'

'No. It is circumstances which are to blame. Who knew

there would be trouble between the Indian government and those Chinese across the border? If the Indian soldiers had not come here in the first place…'

Noora's words trailed off, as she caught Sela gazing quietly at her. Her sister's self-possession and silence, thought the elder girl, were surprising; and commendable. But Sela's eyes seemed to say, 'If the soldiers had not marched into Tawang, I might never have come to know him. And now that I do…'

And then Noora said something that she was to regret for the rest of her life, probably for all eternity. She said to her sister, 'You must take these provisions to the military camp today. Seek him out there, if that is what you want. Listen to your heart. Go.'

The first thing Sela did after her sister had helped her pack and load the sacks full of churpi and meat on her back, before handing her the cans of milk, was to seek out her best friend. Rincin was all too eager to accompany her.

'Keep an eye on my sister,' Noora said to Rincin softly, smoothing the child's hair, 'And bring her back safe.'

Watching her sister and Rincin trudge enthusiastically away over the rocks and meadows in the direction of the camp, Noora was glad to behold Sela's cheerful self, again. But an hour later her happiness turned to apprehension when someone hailed her, and she saw that it was Thabo.

'I have come to speak to your father,' he said without preamble. He entered the house unbidden. 'Where is the old man?'

'In town,' she replied. 'And he will not return for lunch today. So you must not wait.'

He shrugged, 'Well, then…I might as well have a talk with your sister. Matters cannot be allowed to drift like this.'

'I am afraid she isn't home, either.'

Chagrin darkened his face, as he asked, suspiciously, 'Where is she, then? Your father promised...'

'Maybe he did,' snapped Noora. 'But Sela is at the monastery. She has gone there to speak to the Khempo and seek forgiveness for causing father so much pain,' she lied, glibly.

'Has she, indeed?' a hopeful smile twisted his lips, if not his eyes, which were still sceptical, 'That is good. If your sister is beginning to see the error of her ways...you know that I mean her no harm. Is it wrong for a man to want to make a girl his wife?'

'No,' she shook her head, wondering what unseen force had prompted her to speak a blatant falsehood, without batting an eyelid. She was normally a poor liar. 'That is the right thing to do.'

'Well then...' he said, fidgeting and casting glances around the house, as if hoping she would invite him to have some apang beer and snacks. He had been the beneficiary of Noora's exceptional culinary talents, often enough.

On a normal day, she would have been hospitable even to a stranger who came to her door. But now she hated Thabo with all her heart for being the cause of the rift between her father and sister. Her heart quailed, once more, as she recalled the beating Sela had endured, and the deep red welts on her sister's tender, fair skin.

'I...I shall be going, then,' the herder stood up. Then, he lumbered clumsily out of the house, while she stood at her door watching him leave. He had walked only a few steps before he stopped and turned to address her, again. 'I hope the Khempo gives her good advice...and that she takes it. Tell her that I am going to be a very wealthy man, soon. Probably the wealthiest in Tawang. The military have contracted me to supply yaks and mules to them…also porters. They need a lot of those…so…'

'Good for you,' she thought, but said nothing.

❦

Rincin watched her friend and the Indian soldier talking, as if for the two of them nothing else existed in creation. Although she understood that young men and girls do get attracted to one another and sometimes even settle down as man and wife, she found Sela's forwardness quite disgusting. When this tête-à-tête was over, and they were on their way back home, she was going to give Sela a piece of her mind.

Meanwhile, she busied herself with chasing some large, white butterflies across the meadows sprawled around the military camp. She thought she was on the verge of catching one, when a light tap on her shoulder made her look up.

It was a portly soldier in a full-sleeved khaki coloured sweater and khaki shorts, looking down at her. 'What are you doing chasing moths here, little girl? Don't you have a school to go to?'

She didn't quite understand what he was saying, but caught the word 'school', and pointed in the direction of Tawang town. 'There is a school there…but it is too far away, close to the place where my father goes to work. Mother says there is no point wasting so much time walking back and forth.'

Ramratan nodded, only partly comprehending her rapid prattle in the Monpa dialect.

'Come along.' Holding one hand, he led her toward the kitchen. He made her sit down on a bench by a table and laid out some food for her to eat. She was on the point of refusing, when she realized she was hungry. So, she tasted the food. It was delicious, although it was nothing like the food her mother prepared. She began to wolf it down, while the cook watched her with an indulgent gaze. As he did, he took a frayed leather wallet out of the hip pocket of his shorts and gazed at it.

Noticing the cook's preoccupation, Rincin, having polished off the food, hopped over to peek at whatever it was that held his attention.

It was the picture of a little girl, almost Rincin's age by her looks. He said, 'That is my daughter. She goes to school in Dehradun. After the war is over, I will go to her…'

'Dehradun?' She couldn't follow his words exactly, but understood that he was missing the little girl, who was probably his daughter.

'I wish I had a friend like that…' she muttered to herself, while her host slipped the wallet lovingly back into his pocket. 'That Sela is no more trustworthy…oh my god!'

She had recalled suddenly the promise made to Noora, of keeping a close watch on Sela's activities. Without so much as a goodbye or a thank you, the waif sped away to look for her friend, while Ramratan stood scratching his head and smiling wistfully.

He was still wondering, a few minutes later, about why something as awful as war should come to so idyllic a place as these mountains, peopled by inoffensive, affectionate people, when he noticed Jaswant walking slowly up, with a hangdog look on his face.

'What's the matter, Rifleman Jaswant?' Ramratan grabbed the youth by one drooping shoulder. 'Did she say no?'

Jaswant shook his head and sat down upon a bench.

'Want a little tea?' asked the cook, trying to cheer him up. 'Why should you be so glum, my friend? Two pretty sisters…

both eager to feed you paneer and make love to you…'

'Don't you make fun of me!' Jaswant snapped at him.

'Okay, okay…don't fly off the handle, young man. But which one are you going to take to wife, if at all? Have you been able to decide?'

'What do you mean?' demanded Jaswant, glaring at the cook. 'Sela…it is Sela I love. I only speak nicely to the other one because she is her sister.'

Ramratan handed his young colleague a mug of steaming tea and sat down facing him. Together, they sipped the sweet mixture of tea leaves boiled in yak's milk, from their enamel mugs. 'That may be so…but how do you know that girl also is not in love with you? I am ten years older than you, boy, and I have seen much in life. Anything is possible…'

'No. I have given her no such indication. I am sure she knows it is Sela I want.'

'I only hope you never meet one of them on a dark, moonless night,' the cook chuckled, 'They look so much alike… those sisters.'

'Not to me,' snapped Jaswant, slamming his empty cup down and getting to his feet. 'Enough of this…I am going to prepare my uniform.'

'You do that, youngster. We might have to take positions in a bunker anytime now. You will want to look your best when the Chinese come marching in, eh?'

Jaswant's gloom deepened, 'Is it that bad? At the parade this morning, Subedar Udai Singh said Delhi is still talking to the Chinese. The situation might not be as serious as it seems after all.'

'That is if the talks succeed, my boy. Then maybe you can take your bride home when you return for Diwali…that's in a little over ten days…I think. Although…the messages coming from Dhola Post aren't happy…'

The Gam Budha didn't seem too pleased either, sitting hunched in his chair with the radio pressed close to his ears so he could hear at least the brief snatches of information that were audible between prolonged intervals of static. Sela went up to her father and sat at his feet.

'What do you seek in there, father?' she asked. 'Inside that shiny box which makes so much noise…everything is happening here, in and around Tawang. Won't we know about things long before the news reaches those people in Delhi?'

He gazed at her, marvelling at such wisdom in one so young. He nodded, 'You are right, of course. It is all happening here… only a few miles away. The Indian Army is waiting at Dhola and Tsangle and Zimithang. The Chinese watch them from their high citadels on the Thag La ridge. Sometimes, they make announcements over loud hailers, addressing our soldiers and the people of Tawang. Indians and Chinese are brothers, they say. But no one knows what is going to happen, it seems…at the meeting today, everybody was making conjectures…'

'Are you afraid, father?' Sela took her father's callused fingers between her shapely, silken palms and caressed them. 'Don't be. I am not afraid. Nor is Noora…' she raised her voice and called, 'Do you feel scared, sister?'

Noora came up to them, wiping her fingers on a clean rag tucked into the sash around her waist. 'I don't know…I don't know at all. Although the Khempo says men are foolish. They must learn that all men are brothers…whether Chinese, Indians…or Monpas. It is a universal life force that is within and without us, that binds everything together…'

The old man looked at his elder child and nodded, 'I understand what you mean. But…' Then he sighed, a deep, shuddering breath that sent a quiver all through his ageing frame, and he leaned forward to take Sela's face between his palms. Looking into her eyes, he said, 'Will that young man marry you, child? What are his intentions?'

Sela blushed, and hugged her father so tight that he had to struggle to breathe.

'He said today he wants to marry me, father. As quickly as possible…lest the fighting begins and he has to go away…'

He gazed at her, and then at Noora, whose eyes also had a strange light at this moment, which he mistook to be the gleam of maternal affection. She was, in fact, thinking of her soldier. Would he ever tell her something similar, as Sela's lover had done?

'That is what I am afraid of, my children. If you marry a soldier…and he goes into battle…anything can happen. I will not be able to survive your grief, I tell you.'

'Will you be able to watch my sorrow if I spend the rest of my life pining for him?' Sela asked petulantly, her limbs trembling with emotion.

Noora placed a gentle hand on her father's drooping head, 'Are you wondering about what you will say to Thabo?'

At this he reared up, as if roused from a deep sleep, and pulling his daughters close he put both arms around the girls and said, 'No, I am trying to decide how much of a dowry I will be able to give for my daughters. Now Sela…and in due course, you too, my child.'

# 8

The drills, exercises and pep talks were suddenly at an end. It was a clear day in Tawang, though cold. When the orders arrived for 'A' Company to move to a defensive position two kilometres north of Tawang and dig in, the men were excited, to say the least. War is bad, but for a fighting man inactivity is even worse. So, the opportunity to march with a purpose and prepare for battle was just the tonic the battalion needed.

By noon that day, information seeped in about a developing debacle in the Dhola Post sector. The Chinese had attacked in force, at 0500 hours that morning. Of course, the Gorkhas and Rajputs, occupying defensive positions across that front, were reliable. They were the bravest of the brave. So were the Punjabis and Grenadiers, at Tsangle and Hathungla. But the odds, it seemed, were insurmountable even for these regiments accustomed to fighting under terrible conditions. Most of these battalions, everyone knew, were surviving and fighting on hard scales and pouch ammunition, against a far better outfitted, equipped and acclimatized enemy. Still, they were fighting, giving their colleagues at Tawang and beyond the opportunity to strengthen defences and prepare for their time of reckoning, when it arrived.

'What is bothering you?' Gopal carried his plate to where Jaswant was seated, in the battalion mess.

The latter shook his head, 'Nothing.'

'Of course you're out of sorts…don't I know you? A few days ago, you were itching to get at the enemy, and look at yourself now. You seem positively depressed.'

'It's not that…'

'What, then?'

'Fool!' barked Ramratan, ambling over to join the two friends. 'Don't you realize that your friend is lovesick? He's thinking of his beloved, Gopal. He is suffering the pangs of impending separation…isn't that so, Jaswant?'

Jaswant looked earnestly at the cook, 'Tell me, brother… you have spent so much time in the military…over a decade. Isn't that right?'

'Mm…hmm.' Ramratan squinted at his younger colleague, 'What's your point, boy?'

'I was wondering. Does war…has fighting ever solved any problem? Between people…or nations?'

'Wah! Did you hear that? Our Jaswant is turning into a philosopher!' bellowed the cook, clapping on his young colleague's back.

'Coward is more like it, seems to me,' muttered Gopal to Trilok, who had joined them, meanwhile. 'Have you noticed, ever since that girl has come into his life, he's changed. He even doesn't like talking to us…'

'That is what a woman can do to a man, fellers,' chuckled Ramratan. 'As for the charge of cowardice, that is unfair. When a man cares for someone, he doesn't want that person to come to any harm. At the moment, Jaswant is thinking of what will become of his ladylove and her family, should the war come to Tawang. Isn't that so, Jaswant?'

The young rifleman gazed pleadingly at his vastly more experienced colleague, and the look in his eyes gave him away.

'Don't you worry...Gopal and I will go and check on her while you prepare the trenches and bunkers to welcome our Chinese guests,' Trilok winked at Gopal, 'Won't we, Gusain?'

'Of course we will,' chuckled Gopal.

'Tch tch! A pair of fools you are,' snarled the cook, caressing the beginnings of a paunch. 'Look here, my young friends...the fun and games are now at an end. Forget about going anywhere for the next few days. I was chatting with the Subedar a while ago. If our lines at Dhola and Zimithang give, 4 Garhwal will be all that stands between the Chinese and Tawang. So better clean your rifles and take the rust off your bayonets. And eat while you can...without complaining about the water in my dal. Be grateful that you have even this to line your worthless bellies with. Pah!'

Ramratan sauntered away, grumbling about young men who thought soldiering was some kind of a picnic.

'Do you think I could get a couple of hours leave?' Jaswant turned to Gopal.

'You could ask the Jemadar, and he will speak to Subedar Udai Singh,' said Trilok.

'Don't even think of it!' Gopal shook his head, vehemently, 'Not unless you want to get court-martialled for deserting your post, in the middle of a battle.'

'But there's no fighting...yet.'

'He has a point,' said Trilok. 'It's not as if the war has reached Tawang. From what I gather, it is at least one day's march from Dhola and Zimithang to Tawang. That gives our friend time enough to find his beloved. After all, there is also the precedent of a General leaving the battlefield...in the middle of such a major operation.'

'Hush!' said Gopal, tapping Trilok on the head, 'Stop that, you! This is no time for that kind of talk. We're soldiers, not Generals. Remember that...'

'I also will be a Captain,' murmured Jaswant, 'Someday.'

'Not if you don't give up daydreaming, at this point of time. Be patient, Jaswant. I know how you feel. I have a girl too, back in Dehradun. We are to be married when I return home this time. But...what cannot be cured must be endured.'

'That's right,' added Trilok. 'Besides, we pulled through that Nagaland stint, didn't we? These Chinese cannot be worse than those Naga headhunters. Remember that Naga chief you wrestled to the ground and captured?'

'You did teach that yak herder a lesson, too. So, keep your chin up, Jaswant.'

Jaswant looked desolate, 'I wish I hadn't listened to you, that day. If I hadn't wrestled with that man, I might never have...'

Trilok wagged a finger at his despondent friend, while Gopal put a comforting hand across his shoulders. 'Aww...no. Don't blame us, buddy. It is all in the stars. Believe me...if she is destined to become your woman, she will. How dare the Chinese try to stop you, when even the Himalayas can't!'

When Sela visited the military camp that afternoon, carrying the supplies meant for the soldiers' kitchen, it was to find new faces there. Some of the battalion's soldiers, she was told upon enquiring, had been moved to a place a couple of miles out of Tawang. But that was all the information she could elicit from the new cook. This particular man was nowhere near as affable as the one she had met on earlier occasions. He also didn't think it proper to discuss military affairs or troop movements with Monpa girls. These were fraught times, he confided to some of his colleagues, and there was no knowing how many of these locals might shift their loyalties to the Chinese, should the invaders break into Tawang.

'Don't you worry,' Noora reassured her despondent sister, 'Maybe they will come back soon. When father returns from the Indian agent's office after today's meetings, he will be able to tell us all that is going on.'

'I am going to look for Jaswant,' said Sela. 'I cannot bear this suspense any longer.'

Jaswant...so that was Sela's lover's name! Noora wondered at the apprehensions in her own heart, and the fate of her soldier. She still had not discovered his name. Was he also among the soldiers who had been moved to the positions north of Tawang? But she dared not discuss this matter with anyone, least of all, her sister. It was her responsibility to look to her sibling's needs, and those of her father's, before she could think of herself.

So she said to Sela, 'No, it is not safe to wander about the town and the villages, anymore. It will be better if you stay home and prepare meat and churpi. There are also some goral pelts that need cleaning. Let us wait for father to return.'

But it was Thabo who arrived some time later, with the news that the Indians had been defeated at Dhola. His words betrayed a grim satisfaction at this development. The Chinese were going to overrun the Indian positions, he went on. In fact, very soon they might be within striking distance of Tawang.

'The Indians are already recruiting porters to accompany the troops...to carry their equipment so that they can withdraw from here. I look at this as an opportunity for making some money.'

'I am willing to be a porter,' said Sela, immediately.

'Don't be a fool!' Noora chided her sister. 'It is dangerous to be with the soldiers at this time…there is no saying where they will go…or what they will do. Besides, I know that father would never agree.'

'Your sister is right,' said Thabo, gazing steadily at Sela, as if he could divine her reasons for wanting to be a porter with the Indian Army, 'I did not mean that you should get mixed up in those menial jobs. Besides, what is the need for you to work?'

His expression seemed to imply that he was only waiting for her consent, so that he might provide her with a comfortable home, and all conceivable luxuries.

Instead, Sela got to her feet, 'I am not afraid…in fact, I don't mind being a porter for the soldiers!' she snapped, and made for the door as if she were going to rush out of the house that very instant.

'Wait!' Noora hurried after her sibling, dragging her back inside, 'You mustn't do anything foolish…at this stage. Remember what father said. Trust him…'

At this remark of Noora's, Thabo smiled and nodded, with a knowing look, 'I knew the old man would come around. It is not every day that he can find a groom for his daughter who offers five yaks…and doesn't want a dowry either…'

'You must leave now,' Noora turned to the herder, 'Please. We have much work to do, since the winter isn't far away. I will tell father that you called.'

Thabo left reluctantly, but before he plodded off, he couldn't resist saying, 'If the Chinese take over Tawang, they also will need yaks…and porters. And at that time, I will be the most important contractor in Tawang. Remember that. Everyone listens to people with money…and those who can be of use to them.'

No sooner had Sela's persistent suitor left, than Rincin skipped into the house, casting backward glances over her shoulder. 'What did he want?' asked the little girl, 'Haven't you told him yet that you have decided to marry your soldier, Sela? If he is such a wealthy and influential man as he claims to be, he should have no difficulty finding another girl. If you don't tell him, I will…'

'You'll do no such thing!' scolded Noora, tugging gently at one of the ears of the impertinent child, 'Now, stay here with Sela, while I visit the monastery. I must speak to the Khempo urgently.'

'Why…have you also found a soldier for yourself?' asked the child, artlessly.

At which Noora blushed, and hastened to add, 'Little fool… you're imagining things…'

But Sela had noticed her sister's confusion. After Noora left, she asked her friend, 'Do you know who it is that my sister has found for herself? It would be wonderful, wouldn't it…if both of us could be married to two men from the same place. He…Jaswant told me that most of his colleagues are from the villages in a place called Garhwal. In that case, we could live close to each other even after marriage…and visit one another frequently.'

'Ah, but you will be far away from Tawang,' the waif reminded her, 'And what about your father? He will be alone, if both of you leave.'

'You're right,' said Sela, frowning, 'I hadn't thought of that at all. I have been selfish…thinking only of myself. We cannot leave him behind…all alone.'

'Not to worry. I am here. I will come over and see him every day, and make sure that he eats all his meals and takes his rest. I will look after him after you sisters leave. Maybe you can come back once in a while, to visit him…and me.' Suddenly, Rincin looked crestfallen, 'Of course, you might go so far away that you will forget me…'

'Forget you?' exclaimed Sela, and grabbing the child by both arms she clasped her to her breast. 'Never! Do you hear…we…I shall never ever forget you, Rincin. You will still be my best friend, even though he may be my…'

The colour rose to her cheeks, at the thought, and her eyes took on a faraway look.

The child dabbed at her moist eyes, 'Just remember that, Sela. Husbands cannot always be trusted, but friends will always be friends.'

'As if you know anything about husbands,' Sela playfully cuffed her little companion's cheeks.

'I do, too. My father tells me things. He reads books. Don't you know…that is why he is employed at the office of an important officer. Only people who have studied books can work in those offices.'

'So why doesn't he send you to the school in the Indian officials' colony? That will help you grow up to become an important official, eh?'

Rincin nodded, 'That's right. But father says the school is too far away. It is dangerous for little girls to walk that far.'

'So what? We wander all over Tawang,' exclaimed Sela, 'Nothing's ever happened to us…'

'Are you saying that?' Rincin threw her friend a sly glance.

The girls were now busy scraping and cleaning the goral pelts, as Noora had instructed them to. 'You, Sela?'

'Ah, no…that's different.'

'How is it different? Look what happened to you…and your sister!'

'My sister?' Sela was thoughtful for a bit, 'Have you found out who it is that Noora has found for herself? Who is her soldier?'

'How am I to know? I am always with you, or running errands for my mother and the neighbours. But I promise you this…I will find out and tell you.'

'If only Noora would confide in me,' said Sela, wistfully. 'No wonder she's been taking care of her appearance…recently.'

'I have a wonderful idea!' exclaimed Rincin, 'You could both get married at the same time.'

'If that happens, father can stop worrying about his daughters' marriage…and live peacefully.'

'Peace? That's quite another matter. Have you forgotten? There is going to be a war. People are going to die.'

Sela gripped her little friend's shoulder and said, 'No! Don't say that. Maybe we should go to the monastery and pray to the Sakya Muni…that no one dies.'

'But everyone dies, Sela. Sooner or later. Even babies die…sometimes. My father says, it is how you die…and for what reason…that determines whether you have followed the right path.'

# 9

For the soldiers of 'A' Company of 4 Garhwal Rifles, though, the path facing them was far from being a harbinger of clarity, or redemption. They had been told this track, leading from Zimithang and Hathungla, along the Samatso ridge to Tawang, was the most likely route for the Chinese to approach the town.

At the moment, the kutcha road was shrouded in a mist, of vapour and uncertainty. The morning of 23rd October dawned cold and damp—colder than usual. The moisture in the air was more oppressive than ever to the lungs of these soldiers on vigil in the trenches and bunkers on this ridge, two kilometres north of Tawang. Although the Garhwalis, children of the mountains themselves, were used to cold and montane weather, the altitudes and weather of these high Himalayan ridges were a challenge even for them.

At 0900 hrs, Second Lieutenant Tandon addressed his men, announcing, 'It seems the Namka Chu position is lost. The Chinese will be paying us a visit, soon. Remember…not one of us will leave his post, as long as there is a single Chinese soldier left standing or our ammunition lasts. I wish you luck, men. *Jai Badri Vishaal!*'

*'Jai Badri Vishaal!'* echoed 'A' company, as one man.

The Lieutenant and Subedar Udai Singh then went on a round of the defensive positions, making sure the men were alert, and in as good spirits as could be, under the circumstances.

Jemadar Pratap Singh's platoon was at the forefront and likely to receive the brunt of the enemy's shells, which the Chinese were sure to rain down upon them before their infantry advanced. The men were checking their rifles one more time, and their ammunition pouches. Another round of tea was served, this time with salt, because the Company had run out of sugar. Still, at this altitude, it was better than nothing; and in the cold, the steaming liquid laced with a suggestion of yak's milk was no less than an elixir.

Jaswant, in one of the trenches directly facing the likely enemy approach route, chose this moment to unbutton the pocket of his khaki flannel shirt and take out the unfinished letter to his mother. But his fountain pen was out of ink. Answering his best friend's enquiring gaze, Gopal Gusain shook his head as if to say, 'No, I am not carrying a pen...'

But at that moment, the Lieutenant and Subedar arrived on their rounds, and both the riflemen snapped to their feet, saluting smartly.

'At ease, Gopal...Jaswant...' said the Lieutenant, smiling grimly as he noticed the inland letter in Jaswant's fist. 'You are an optimist...to be writing a letter at this time. We might never make it out of here alive, do you know?'

'But this letter might, Saabji,' said Jaswant, resolutely, looking his Company Commander in the eye.

'Well, yes...maybe. Go ahead then,' the officer placed an encouraging hand on the rifleman's shoulder, 'Write your letter and hand it over to Udai Singh before the battle begins. I know somehow…that my Subedar will survive. Our JCOs are the most difficult to kill, you see…'

Everyone smiled, including the Subedar, but Jaswant's gaze was fixed on the Lieutenant's shirt's pocket, 'Can I borrow that pen, Saabji? I'll return it…to Subedar Saheb…'

'You don't have to, Jaswant,' the officer laughed, briefly, plucking the writing instrument from his pocket, 'This was a gift from my father, when I received my commission. You keep it, now. Let this be my Diwali gift to the wrestling champion of our battalion. There's nothing else we can give you…at this point. I understand you won a bout against a local hero, a few days ago? I am only sorry I missed the action…'

'I…I'm sorry, Saabji…I didn't mean to…' Jaswant stuttered in confusion.

'You don't have to apologize for keeping the Indian Army's flag flying high, my friend. Go on, now…finish your letter. The Chinese will be here any minute now, and I don't want my men distracted by thoughts of their families…in the middle of a fight.'

But the Chinese, it seemed, were in no hurry. Sporadic reports trickling through to the Garhwalis via Divisional headquarters indicated the invaders were busy mopping up the remnants of the Indian 7 Infantry Brigade, which they had overwhelmed at the battle of Namka Chu. With their communication lines having been severed, there was very little information available about the fate of the Brigade, except that it had disintegrated.

Every man of 'A' Company was raring to have a go at the marauding Chinese, to avenge their unfortunate but brave Sikh and Rajput comrades of Dhola. But to the Lieutenant's chagrin, orders arrived at precisely 1030 hours for the company to withdraw to Tawang, forthwith. There had been a change of plans. HQ 4 Artillery Brigade, of which the Garhwalis had become a part since their deployment to Tawang, would be abandoning the town. According to the morning's orders, 4 Garhwal Battalion was tasked with covering the withdrawal of the HQ and other units from Tawang to Se La, by the Jang road.

'At this rate we'll never get to fight!' Jaswant burst out, when the Subedar informed his troops about the latest orders.

For a moment, the veteran glared at his dissenting rifleman, as if he would brook no insubordination among the troops, whatever the provocation. Then he shrugged, and poked a finger at Jaswant, 'Your turn will come.'

'Are you itching to be locked up in the quarter guard?' Lance Naik Trilok Negi asked his friend, when the Subedar had left to discuss with the Company Commander the plans for the retreat to Tawang.

'We've been here two weeks already,' murmured Jaswant, 'And all we are doing is cooling our heels and putting on weight, while our more fortunate colleagues in the other battalions corner all the glory. We Garhwalis are as brave as anyone else...'

'There's no need to prove that,' Trilok mollified his friend.

'Look at the bright side, Jaswant. We're returning to Tawang...and that gives you an opportunity to...' Gopal intervened at this point, emphasizing his meaning with a wink, 'you know what I mean.'

'Of course he knows what you mean!' sniggered Negi. 'I only hope all the Monpas haven't already fled Tawang...'

'They can't...they won't...' Jaswant blurted out.

'Then this is your opportunity, Jaswant,' Gopal took his friend aside, 'Once we reach Tawang, look for your girl. I'll try and cover for you...somehow. Speak to her...if you can, make her your wife. This might be your last opportunity...'

'Don't say that...Gopal!'

'It's not me saying anything. Didn't you hear the Lieutenant and the Subedar? It is the Chinese who are calling the shots here...and our confused leaders,' Rifleman Gusain left the thought hanging in the chill air of Samatso, as 'A' Company gathered their equipment and prepared for the trek back to Tawang.

People were getting ready to travel to neighbouring places; those in the little *basha* huts of the villages scattered around Tawang, as well as in the homes lining the alleys of the hamlet. Perhaps the Indian officials and their families who lived in the Assistant Political Officer's colony were leaving Tawang without any regrets, because now they would be able to return to the plains and other parts of India that they hailed from. But for the many who were born and had grown up here, basking in the unrestrained sunlight bathing the mountains, drinking of the pellucid streams that poured all year long into the sedately flowing Nyamjang Chu and the cascading rapids of the Tawang Chu, departure was like death.

Despite the seeming economic opportunity offered by hundreds of soldiers milling around the area at this time, the natives of Tawang were a bewildered community. The Monpas were a peaceful people, with their lives ordered around the great monastery and its comforting rituals, which only embellished the drudgery of interminable, daily chores. Still, at this time, even they might have fought and died to protect their homes, if only someone would lead them into the fight.

But nothing of the kind was happening. The soldiers, the professional warriors in whom the population of Tawang had reposed faith all these weeks, were abandoning them to their fate. With a terse, 'Tawang cannot be defended...the Chinese will encircle us here...' the Generals of the Indian Army had washed their hands off this faraway hamlet, which after all was nothing like the electrified towns and hectic cities that defined a growing nation, and therefore, deserved protection. The remnants of 7 Infantry Brigade's decimated units, besides whatever battalions of the Division remained intact, would retreat in an orderly manner to Se La, which according to the higher powers was far more advantageous for a pitched battle.

When Rincin arrived with the news that her father had decided their family also should abandon Tawang, Noora didn't know what to say. The child was almost in tears, at the thought of leaving her life here and her best friend. On the other hand, though, she could not suppress the childish excitement of going to new places, gaining new experiences. 'Father says his officer has invited us to Delhi. There, father can keep his job, and I will be able to go to a proper school.'

'Then maybe you should go,' said Noora, seemingly busy in her kitchen. But her thoughts were elsewhere. As for the best friend Rincin was loath to leave, that companion appeared not even to have acknowledged her arrival. Noora's sister stood at the door of their little home, gazing out into the sunshine.

'What's the matter with her?' asked Rincin. 'She hasn't even spoken to me...is she really so enamoured of that soldier? I thought they were playing a game...'

'Shh!' hissed Noora, glancing at her father hunched in his chair. Apparently, he was still trying to gather news from the radio that now was spewing only static. It was as if the gadget had become a lifeline for the old man, a beacon of some undefinable hope.

That hope was extinguished when Thabo lumbered in some

time later, with a gleam in his eyes that belied the lugubrious expression on his deeply sun-browned features. 'The Indians don't stand a chance,' he said, sitting down beside the old man, although he kept his gaze upon the girls, looking from Sela to Noora, as if daring either one of them to contradict his verdict.

Sela turned and marched up to her sister with a determined look, 'I am going to the flea market to sell some of that meat and churpi. We'll still need money and provisions to get by, won't we? This isn't the end of the world.'

'And maybe you will find there the flame that will light your new world,' thought Noora to herself. She was on the point of refusing, for fear that their parent would be upset by Sela venturing out of doors at this delicate time, when Rincin said, 'Do let us go, Noora. I will accompany Sela and bring her back safe, I promise. I will be going away after all…soon. Who knows when I shall return.'

Noora ruffled the little one's hair, while her eyes watched Thabo and her father out of the corners of her eyes. The old man was distracted, and he didn't seem to realize or care what was going on, even as Thabo fixed the girls with a baleful look.

'Don't stay out too long,' said Noora to her sister.

Minutes after this injunction, the two girls tripped out of the house, with Sela carrying the satchels containing her merchandise. Noora leaned against the door jamb and watched them skipping away, across the hillside. When they were quite out of sight, she sighed, shook her head and returned to attend to her remaining chores. It was then she realized that in her anxiety to leave, Sela had even forgotten to take her cap with her. Noora plucked it off the nail on the wall and gazed at the yak skin headgear with its brightly coloured plume, when Thabo intruded upon her thoughts, with, 'I can go and find her. I mean… I can hand the cap over to your sister.'

'Maybe she left it at home on purpose,' snapped Noora, trying to keep the edge out of her words.

'Very well, then. Perhaps I *should* go out there anyway, and make sure the girls don't get into any kind of trouble. Things are very uncertain now. I don't trust the Indians at all…'

'But you were offering them your yaks?' she couldn't help asking.

He gave one of his rare, uneasy smiles, 'That is business. I will do as much for the Chinese, when they reach Tawang. Everybody likes to deal with a good businessman. I believe it is in the interests of all of us to befriend the Chinese. That way, they will not harm our families…and we can also trade with them. You know, even they need porters and provisions.'

'I wish you luck with your business,' she said and turned away, while he cast one despairing glance at the old man, who was still glued to the indecipherable radio noises, then laboured out of the house.

Noora waited a couple of hours, pottering about the house and in the small kitchen garden outside, after she had completed the day's chores. Or perhaps it was because she was too nervous to carry on like this, with all the uncertainty. She knew that Sela's trip to the market was inspired by the hope of running into some Indian soldiers, maybe even her Jaswant. Where, she wondered, was her own soldier at that moment? Was he still in Tawang, or had he already left for Se La, with his colleagues? She understood it was unlikely that any soldier worth his salt would linger and desert his troop for a girl at a time like this, with the enemy pursuing them and more battles to come. So she comforted herself with the advice the Khempo had once given her, 'As surely as the sun rises every morning, my child, so must we, who live off his warmth, believe that the wheel of life will turn and our beloved ones will return to us...'

'Fetch your sister,' said the old man suddenly, interrupting her musings. She looked at him as he continued, 'If she has found her man, it is good. I wish them well. That is all I can do at the moment. Maybe later, after all this is over...'

Her father's face was expressionless, if anything, as he spoke, although he seemed to be in possession of his faculties.

'As for me,' he continued, picking up his stick and walking slowly into the daylight outside the house, 'I will not leave this place. Let them come...who will...Indians or Chinese. Men of war...or those who want peace.'

Noora went up to him, and putting her arms around the ageing frame, she hugged him. Then, she went back in, wore her cap, and picking up her sister's pheasant plume headgear, she hurried off to look for Sela and her inseparable crony. The few dark clouds drifting across the pale blue horizon might gain moisture enough to precipitate later in the day; though not too heavily, she reckoned. Rain, in any case, was a good omen.

# 10

'A' Company were back in Tawang at 1500 hrs. But they kept marching. Already, the Chinese artillery had opened up, and small arms fire buzzed like hornets about the recently abandoned Indian posts. It was the enemy making sure that there was no opposition left on the Samatso ridge.

The jawans were now seated in grim but disciplined rows, four deep, as the Company Commander addressed them. A three-man patrol under Jemadar Gabar Singh sent out to scout the Company's path of retreat had not returned.

'I need volunteers,' said the Lieutenant.

'I will go, Saabji!' Rifleman Jaswant Singh Rawat sprang to his feet.

The Lieutenant stared at his soldier for one long moment, as if he understood why. But he shrugged, and was on the point of saying something when Gopal Gusain also got up, 'I'll go with him, Saabji.'

'One way or another, you will report at Jang by 0930 hrs on the 24th,' Subedar Udai Singh briefed the volunteers, before letting them leave. He had turned down Trilok Negi's request to join Jaswant and Gopal with a curt, 'This isn't a picnic. Two men are just about all I can spare.'

Tawang was beginning to resemble a ghost town, at least the parts which had been populated by the Political Officer's staff and associated establishments. There was also a steady trickle of natives leaving with their families and belongings loaded on mules and yaks.

'Do you know where she lives?' asked Gopal, at which Jaswant looked at his friend as if he couldn't believe his ears.

'Why…why are you looking at me like that, eh? Isn't that why you volunteered, so you could meet her one last time?'

There was an eloquent pause, as Jaswant gazed steadily at his friend, before saying with an easy smile, 'I suppose I can't blame you for thinking that, Gopal. But the thought hadn't crossed my mind, when I volunteered to search for the Jemadar and the others.'

'It's not as if I am blaming you, Jaswant. It would be only natural…'

'No. I know Sela. She will find me, wherever I am. Whether I am dead or alive. That is natural. As for me, I am at this moment a soldier, and my duty is to my colleagues and my nation.'

'We understand that…all of us…'

'Maybe our senior officers don't,' Jaswant sounded angry. 'Why didn't we stay here in Tawang and fight? We were well entrenched, our defences were solid, we could have given a good account of ourselves here… I'm certain.'

Gopal chuckled, 'Oh, so now Brigade and Division will take advice from riflemen, will they?' He patted his friend's back, 'Take it easy, Jaswant. You must realize one thing about the Army. Headquarters is always right. The sooner you learn that the better.'

'Okay, okay. I know the drill. Now, we don't have much time to find our men and get back to the Company. Let's not waste any of it.'

'You're the boss, Jaswant. You have spent more time gallivanting about this place than anyone of us, thanks to that lady. So, where do we begin looking for them?' They were on the periphery of the APO complex, which housed the offices and residences of the Indian government's staff.

'We could start by scouring this entire area, in case the Jemadar and his men went to investigate the situation at the administrative offices…to explore whether some worthwhile defences can be set up there'

'But we're not holding Tawang.'

'Gabar Singh didn't know that. So he was probably looking for places to defend, where we could stall the enemy, inflict maximum casualties.'

'You may be right…'

'I know I'm right, Gopal. Now, there is also the area around the monastery…but that place is crowded, with lots of houses clustered together…narrow alleys…'

'I know,' said Gopal, nodding, 'But all that will take too much time, and we have to be in Jang tomorrow morning. Why don't we split up instead, and meet at the old campsite at 2100 hours. Even if we cannot find transport, we may be able to leg it to Jang by tomorrow morning and join the company. It is 1600 hours now, and that gives us five hours to search. I will start with this area, and you begin with the monastery complex…'

'All right,' Jaswant nodded. Their eyes exchanged a tacit acknowledgement of the fact that Gopal was letting his friend spend more time in the areas surrounding the monastery, which was where they had first met Sela at the wrestling match. Maybe the girl's home was close by.

They embraced before parting.

❦

Today was the monthly market day, when traders, from as far as Bhutan, would come to Tawang to buy and sell. Naturally, the place was more crowded than usual. The throng only made it more difficult for Noora to locate her sister. Fortunately, a large number of her acquaintances were there. While some people were stocking up in preparation for the impending invasion, others were trying to sell off as much of their produce as they could, for there was no knowing when another such opportunity was likely to present itself.

Some people had, indeed, seen Sela and Rincin at the market. A few had even chatted with the girls, which wasn't surprising considering her sister's appetite for conversation. But for the life of them, not one of these acquaintances could quite recall whether Sela was still around, or in which direction she had gone. In any case, she was a flighty girl, and there was no knowing where she might be at this moment, or whose leg she might be pulling.

At some point, Noora even had the impression that she sighted Thabo in the crowd. She knew that he was a very well-known figure about Tawang, and kept himself informed about everything that went on in the town and the villages. But she was in no mood to speak to him at the moment, let alone touch a raw nerve by asking him about Sela, and so she melted quickly into the stream of people so that he might not see or hail her.

The afternoon was far advanced and the sky thickening with moisture. The pleasant breeze of the morning was now a cold wind. Although she was exhausted from all the walking and enquiring, she did not wish to return home without Sela. It never once occurred to her that her sister might have gone back home, while she was out looking for her. She felt, instinctively, that Sela would take this opportunity to reach out to her Jaswant. There had been that determined glint in her eyes when she left home, without even her cap. That was an omission she would never make, unless her mind were fixated on some other, grand notion.

On an impulse, Noora decided that she should spend a few minutes at the monastery. There was the chance, though slim, that Sela would be there to seek the Lord's blessings.

Today Noora did not exchange pleasantries with the lamas as they went about their chores inside the gompa. Even the ascetics, she noticed almost absent-mindedly, were not their cheerful selves. There was a new anxiety in their steps when the red and ochre clad servants of the faith hurried past her, and their greetings communicated a strange restlessness that almost mirrored the tumult within her, rather than their customary affability and quietude.

As it turned out, Sela *had* visited the monastery. But that was several hours ago, said the Khempo. 'What is the matter with your sister?' asked the senior monk, looking thoughtful, 'I have never seen her behave so strangely. Do you know that she stayed here for close to half an hour and lit several lamps and joss sticks…that isn't like her. She is the eternal butterfly… here one moment, gone the next.'

'I worry about her, holy one,' said Noora to the monk.

'Don't. She is what she is. As you are what the divine spirit made you. She will find her way…as you must yours.'

'I…don't know, father…whether I can find the right path…'

'Then you must meditate…and look inward,' said the

servant of the Enlightened One, and moved away to light the large candles, because by now the needles of sunlight streaming into the cavernous shrine were almost gone. Thunder sounded, distant yet portentous.

Noora rose and went around the *dukhang*, the main prayer hall, chanting '*Om Mani Padme Hum*' seven times while she spun the prayer wheels set into the walls. Afterwards, she lit some joss sticks at the altar, and sat down to contemplate the huge feet of the gold painted, thirty-foot high figure of Tomba Sakya Dawa.

'Get back home quickly,' said the Khempo, returning to give a benediction, 'That sounds like a cloudburst. You don't want to be out of doors when it is dark and raining.'

When she bowed, he said, 'May you find what you seek, my child. I will pray.' As she stepped out of the gompa, a sudden, jagged streak of lightning split the evening, and the incandescence illuminated even the inside of the shrine, such that for a fleeting moment she was able to look upon the golden, composed visage of Sakya Muni. For her, this was an omen, and in her heart of hearts she knew the Khempo had spoken the truth. She was going to find Sela presently, because she had come looking for her, seeking her sister's safety and happiness.

But then a voice spoke from the inmost recesses of her being. 'Is that what you seek?'

She panicked, seeing it was almost like night outside. Grey, brooding clouds were gathering overhead. Hurrying home, running and stumbling, she prayed frantically that Sela would be home and dry. In her anxiety to get back to the house, she decided to take a shortcut, and veered off the road on to a *mithun* track. The clouds were so laden with rain; they seemed to be within arm's reach. For a while, the wind buffeted her, slowing her progress. Then, as suddenly as it had developed, the gale dissipated. Everything became still around her, and she picked her way over rock and through bramble, almost tearing her chemise amid the rhododendron bushes in her frantic progress. She knew this calm was too good to last.

She was right. She was still far from home, with no idea how far or whether she had strayed, when the wind started up again, picking up speed. One powerful gust caught her, making her lose her footing on the animal track so that she went tumbling down the mountainside. Her fall was broken by the protruding trunk and roots of a large tree. She grabbed hold of a jutting root, gasping for breath, holding on for dear life. The road was somewhere below, how many feet away she could not judge. The wind was howling and shrieking like a demon now. Even if she called for help, no one was likely to hear. In the darkness, she could not even see where she was. It started to rain. Soon, her clothes were drenched. Within moments, sheets of water were cascading down the rocks and meadows. This torrent rushed downhill, sweeping everything in its path, stone and brush and mud. The slush poured over her, covering her from head to toe and seeping through her chemise and blouse. For some reason, she held on to Sela's cap that was still in her right fist, clutching frantically to the plumed yak skin headgear as if her life depended on it. She felt her grip slipping because of the slush that also covered the tree root she was grasping. She prayed silently, recalling the Sakya Muni's unwavering countenance. Somehow, the face smiled at her through the choking slush, and she marvelled at the clipped, straight moustache that had materialised miraculously over the Blessed One's full lips.

# 11

Jaswant spent a couple of hours scouting the localities close to the monastery. He didn't deem it wise to go around asking people about the Jemadar's whereabouts. Given the state of affairs in and around Tawang, the Chinese might already have their spies casing the town. In any case, if his colleagues were in this area, which seemed unlikely given its location and layout, they would show up sooner or later.

He could not help a twinge of guilt, realizing that he was equally anxious, perhaps more so, to locate Sela. Here again, the prospect of enemy agents deterred him from enquiring of the local population about her residence, or her present whereabouts.

More on an impulse than with any real hope of finding her there, he entered the monastery compound. His eyes took in the tall portals, the great, elaborately carved roof of the gompa, its spire that gleamed even in the murky light of the afternoon. He glanced quickly at the threatening skies, dreading the prospect of heavy rain. That would only make his quest that much more difficult. Becoming suddenly conscious of the rifle slung on his shoulder, and that this was an abode of peace, he was on the point of turning away when he heard someone calling.

He turned to see a lama at the great doors, beckoning to him to enter. Drawn as if by a powerful hand reaching out from the inside of the shrine, he followed the lama inside. The ascetic motioned to him to sit down near the feet of the Sakya Muni. He did, removing and placing his hat and rifle on the floor by his side.

The lama went away to light some more joss sticks, and returned with the Lord's blessing for this unexpected devotee. Although Jaswant could make nothing of the man's words, he assimilated the sentiment, and bent down to touch his feet, at which the lama stepped back hurriedly and indicated that he should touch the Blessed One's feet, instead. Jaswant complied, and immediately felt a kind, gentle hand being placed upon his head. That touch filled him with a feeling of peace, of eternity he had never experienced before.

By the time he left the monastery, it had started to rain. He hurried off into the darkness, shining the torch from time to time so that he wouldn't lose his way and wander off the principal paths. But in the gloom and fury of the rain it was all he could do to keep walking.

He was struggling to extricate himself from some rhododendron thickets that he had inadvertently walked into, when a faint sound reached his ears. It was distinct from the crash of thunder, the drumming of rain on rocks and leaves. He tried to ignore the distraction and focus on finding his way out of the trackless hillside he seemed to be traversing. Although the darkness and weather were fit to make a person lose all sense of time, he was conscious of the need to get to the rendezvous with Gopal by 2100 hours. He was a soldier, above all...he felt for his rifle, touched its reassuring contours and moved on.

Again, he heard the sighing and scraping. This time it

was perceptible, despite the noise of the cloudburst, probably because it was close at hand. He switched on his torch, directing its beam in the direction from which he thought the sound originated. He hoped that if it was a wild animal, the beast would be blinded by the sudden, dazzling light and take to its heels.

Gradually, as his eyes got used to the brilliance of the beam, he realized it was a tree he was gazing at. It was, in fact, the base of a massive tree growing out of the hillside. Even as he was trying to make sure he wouldn't lose his footing due to the streams of slush swirling around his ankles, he glimpsed a streak of colour against that unrelieved expanse of mud and water. That was...a feather. A brilliant, multicoloured pheasant plume. It had been washed clean by the rain. Then he heard the sound, again. Was that...the sound of a person gasping... for breath?

The plume...the breathing. In the very moment that realization struck, he was leaning forward to grab the pair of slush coated hands that held on desperately to one of the giant's roots. Then, he beheld the pair of eyes, now fear crazed, now hopeful, now closing as if accepting the inevitable.

Thrusting the torch into his belt, he reached forward, grabbed the arms, and with an almighty heave pulled her all the way up, so that her mud-spattered figure came burgeoning out of that gloom and rain and fell upon him. They held on to one another, fearful of letting go, of losing one another again.

'You...it's you...' he said hoarsely.

All that she could do was sob uncontrollably and cling to him, as he got to his feet and made sure that his rifle was secure on his back. His breath fanned her bedraggled, mud streaked hair, and she knew she was safe. 'What in God's name were you doing down there, on that treacherous hillside? What if I hadn't happened along…what if you had been hurt…or broken some bones? Have you no consideration for my feelings?'

He was about to set her gently down, on her feet, when a shudder ran through her frame, soaked as she was in rain and slush and the sweat of fear. He felt the sensation and said, 'No, no… don't worry. I shall not put you down. Don't be afraid. I have come to you, haven't I?'

He started to walk, and she opened her eyes. But her gaze met only the murkiness of the path in front. She dared not look at his face, into his eyes.

Did he know that it was she, Noora? Of course, he did. Would he have saved anyone else in that situation? Of course he would…he was a soldier.

Then, she recalled the smiling face of the Sakya Muni, the moustache, and her fingers lifted to feel his face…this wasn't the Enlightened One…it was the one who had brought an ineffable light into her life…she realized she still didn't know his name. It didn't matter, he was her soldier. As if in reassurance he squeezed her body, still cradled in his powerful sinews, and she let go of that fleeting thought. She wanted only to sense him, to be close to him…always.

With the sureness that only a soldier can have, he walked towards a dilapidated basha on the roadside. It appeared to have been abandoned, after a landslide, by its original owners. But the partially collapsed structure was still adequate refuge for these two, seeking shelter from the storm.

'What did you have to come out in this weather for? See how bad it is! Why don't you speak?' Then he sighed, 'It's just as well. You do most of the talking anyway…whenever we meet…'

No, she wanted to tell him. I love to listen to you speak.

The sound of your voice is so restful. I could listen…forever.

He went on, 'Today, it is I who will speak…to my heart's content. You just listen. Lie in my arms and hear everything that I have to say.'

Noora could not have heard sweeter words. This was precisely what she wanted, to rest in his comforting embrace and hear him talk…and talk. What he said was not important. The mere sound of his voice, his masculine tones droning in the dark, spread an ethereal peace within her.

They were inside the shack now, and he found a haystack in a corner that had somehow withstood the fury of the landslide. He laid her gently upon the hay and stretched himself beside her.

'I could not have gone away from here without meeting you…once.'

Could this be true? There was also a part of Noora that wanted to believe his words, and as his fingers touched her, roaming over face and lips, tracing the contours of her smooth yet parched throat before probing tentatively across her shoulders and breasts, she closed her consciousness to all else but his presence. She was in love.

A small voice shrilled in a corner of her mind, reminding that she had set out to look for Sela earlier that afternoon, and she was being remiss in her duty. But that was before her soldier came to her in the darkness and the rain, yearning to take her in his arms, even as she had ached to melt in his embrace.

He was slipping the sinka gown off her shoulders, releasing her breasts. She wanted to tell him, 'I am dirty, covered in mud'. But he didn't seem to care. He kissed her bare skin, still moist from the soaking, and she shivered. He trembled, too, and laughed softly. Vaguely, she heard him say, 'This is war, my darling…we may not meet again, for a while…'

'Mmm...' she smiled into the darkness, her face grinding into his comforting shoulder.

'We are withdrawing from Tawang. I'm sorry...I didn't want that. If it had been up to me and my compatriots, we would not yield an inch of land to the Chinese. My battalion was sworn to make Tawang the graveyard of the enemy. I hate this waiting...this suspense. It is a soldier's duty to fight...and die!'

'Shh!' she hissed aloud, clapping one palm over his mouth. 'Shh...'

'All right. All right,' his arms tightened about her. 'I will not die. I shall return from the battle, if there is one. I won't die until we have married...had many children. Did you know? We were going to celebrate Dussehra at Tezpur on the 8th October. But we were already in Tawang by the eighth of this month, digging trenches and building walls...preparing for battle... Hey, are you paying attention to what I'm saying?'

'Mmm!' she intoned, and clasped him fast, 'Mmm!'

He chuckled quietly and went on, 'It is good to have a woman listen, for once...instead of talking...'

She closed her eyes and drifted off, letting him continue to talk and make love with his body and his hands. When he started to move inside her she came fully, pleasurably awake.

He was saying, 'Do you know, it is not such a bad thing that we came here. A General Saab visited 4th Brigade Headquarters. He is the Corps Commander, I think. The General has announced an extra allowance for men serving at high altitudes. That includes us...4 Garhwal. So what if we didn't get to celebrate Dussehra? Maybe...maybe I can save money to buy mother a shawl, when I go home. Whenever that is. We were to go home for Diwali, do you know? But now... whenever the fighting is over...will you...will you go with me?'

As the wind howled like an escaping devil outside the squashed hut, Jaswant's words became loud and hoarse, too. 'Will you go, no, come to me? Be mine…mine alone…my… Sela…my Sela… How I love you…my Sela…'

As he babbled on in his frenzy, Noora's wandering senses stilled. For a moment, the blood ran cold in her veins. He seemed to sense her sudden tightening, for he urged, 'What? What is it, my darling? Are you angry with me? But I am going away…didn't you want me as I wanted you…my Sela…' and he began to take her again, frantic with desire.

Noora's last reservations dissolved under that welcome assault. Soon, she was floating far, far away through the valleys between the ridges, up into the mountains and down again, rising and falling. She forgot time…herself…her sister…Sela…

# 12

At this point Mrs Ralte began to weep, and her audience also seemed quite moved by the turn the story had taken.

'Maybe we should stop here,' said Akash, seeing that the lady seemed in no condition to continue. 'Things have been proceeding rather quickly…and maybe we all need some time to reflect…'

'There is also a phone call from the Adjutant, Saabji,' said the orderly, handing Akash his cell phone.

The Lieutenant spoke briefly to his superior, and then turned to Mr Ralte, 'It seems we will need to take a break here, Sir. That was Major Bhagwani. Something important has come up. I must report to the Adjutant's office right away.'

The Gram Pradhan nodded, 'That is quite all right, Lieutenant Akash ji. It is kind of you to have been so patient. Also, maybe my wife could do with some rest now.'

The Adjutant looked closely at Akash, his face lined with obvious scepticism, 'I understand you have been talking to one of the Gram Pradhans, Lieutenant?'

'Yes, Sir. The Pradhan…er…his wife has considerable knowledge of what happened in 1962, I believe…'

'You...believe? And what did she tell you?'

'Well...er...it seems there were two girls, Sir, named Noora and Sela.'

'And they fought and won the war, is that it?'

'Of course not, Sir. No, Sir. It's a fact we lost the war, so that wouldn't be...'

The Adjutant shrugged, 'Well, now...Lieutenant. I told you. These villagers and poorly educated people are easily taken in by such stories, huh? You don't want to give too much credence to everything you hear.'

'I...I'll keep that in mind, Sir. But if the objective is to know the truth about what actually happened back then, we should...'

'You'd better not tell me what we should or shouldn't be doing, young man,' said the Major with a dismissive gesture. 'As for the objective, I've already told you what it is. It is to bide our time, at the same time keeping the local population in good humour, and eventually to send a memorandum to... well, I don't need to repeat those instructions, do I?'

'No, Sir!' Akash clicked his heels and saluted, 'I'll keep that in mind, Sir. No more stories of any kind...'

At this, the Major wagged a finger, 'Oh, no, Lieutenant. That's not what I meant. Listen to everything that anyone tells you...but the important thing is, keep your own counsel. You report back here, and we decide what is true and what's not, savvy?'

Akash appeared to be on the horns of a dilemma, the following morning, as if he were trying to decide how much weight to give to the events that had been described to him the previous day, when the Lance Naik entered and announced, 'I have the jeep ready, Sir.'

'Jeep? Whatever for...where are we going?'

'To Nuranang, Saabji...Jaswantgarh. I though Mr Ralte informed you, Saabji.'

Akash nodded, 'Ah, yes...he did. But...I don't know...' The Gram Pradhan had called on his mobile to inform him that they should meet at the Jaswantgarh shrine the following morning. He had persuaded his wife that they should be at the spot, where she would continue her retelling of those events of a long time ago.

'Are you worried about what the Adjutant Saab said, Saabji?' the orderly smiled, although he was in earnest, 'I think we should go to Nuranang, Saabji...and hear the lady out. It can do no harm, and it will make the Pradhan happy...and the people of Tawang. Isn't that what we want?'

'Well...er, yes...I suppose so.'

Despite his superior's injunction to maintain a healthy dose of scepticism, the Lieutenant couldn't quite help the rush of blood through his veins, as his eyes took in the burst of colour surrounding the pristine white of the Jaswantgarh shrine. The rainbow shades were contrived by pennants of the Indian Army's legendary regiments—Madras, Rajputana, Sikhs, Gurkhas, the Sappers—fluttering in a circle over the walls of the complex. As if providing stark contrast to the reminders of war were the picturesque, pacifist murals and models from Buddhist lore, which studded the inner surfaces of the walls and lined the stairs of the cenotaph.

He now experienced a strange turmoil as he climbed the stairs, although he put it down to the altitude sickness that was common in these parts, and the journey uphill from Tawang to Nuranang. Once inside the memorial, a spotlessly clean room, his orderly announced, 'This is all the martyr's memorabilia, Saabji. That uniform, a pair of shoes, everything belongs to...

Baba. Do you know, Saabji, the bed is made every night, and every morning the sentry finds the sheets rumpled, as if someone has been...'

Akash recalled stopping at the memorial on his first journey up from Bomdi La to Tawang. But he hadn't paid much attention then, and he had been exhausted from the drive.

Now, as the jawan's voice droned on, Akash was looking at the gleaming bronze bust, set on a column in the centre of the room. His eyes fell on the polished brass plate beneath the sculpted replica. '4 GARH RIF' it said. Etched on the marble pedestal beneath was a brief, telegraphic retelling of Rifleman 4039009's courage.

Was it the spirit of this man...martyr...which intervened on the Thandrong pasture?

'*Baba ka Prasad*, Saabji,' said his assistant, almost shouting into the Lieutenant's ear in his excitement at being the bearer of the Baba's benediction, even if it was only a paper cup of saccharine sweet, near-boiling tea from a steel can placed strategically on a table by the roadside at the memorial. As if tea requires any explanation, or pretext, in this cold and at such an elevation.

But he needed to concentrate on the job at hand, such as it was. Besides, he did not wish his companions to think he was being inattentive to their tales of a generation past. After all, as the Adjutant put it, 'Sadbhavana' was the name of the game.

'Where are they...' he glanced at the Lance Naik, who pointed.

'Up there...Saabji...there are a couple of bunkers out there.'

The Gam Pradhan and his wife were indeed seated on the grass outside one of the bunkers. Akash noted, with surprise, that the woman showed none of the distress of the previous day.

He cast a quick glance around the hills surrounding the memorial, his mind speculating about what the conditions might have been like here, forty years ago.

That war had been fought in October-November. The broken slopes girding the memorial, where the martyr had made his last stand, were now carpeted with the fine, green grass of peace. It would have been much colder then, he reckoned, incalculably more adverse.

As if reading his thoughts, he heard someone say, 'That was a very cold, rainy winter…'

With a start, Akash realized that the woman was speaking.

# 13

When darkness fell early, accompanied by the threat of a storm, Gopal decided to give up his seemingly fruitless search for the Jemadar and the other two soldiers, and made for the erstwhile campsite, which was to be his point of rendezvous with Jaswant at 2100 hours. In any case, he did not know the topography of Tawang as well as his friend, and there was every possibility of his getting lost in the darkness. He rationalized that the Jemadar had two men with him, and if they were alive, they would make it back to the battalion eventually. It was more important for him and Jaswant to survive and return.

When the skies opened up a while later, Gopal was glad of his decision.

He would wait out the rain inside one of the log huts the battalion had constructed upon arrival in Tawang. He entered a hut, found a hurricane lantern in one corner with oil in it, and was able to light it with the matches he carried. Peering at his watch in the weak, yellow glow of the lantern, he saw it was still only 1800 hours—he had three hours more to wait for Jaswant to return. There was the possibility, of course, that his friend also might abandon his search early and make for this place. But that seemed unlikely, if he understood Jaswant.

As if to contradict his judgement there was a sudden, frantic knocking at the door of the hut. That might be Jaswant. Yet, he was taking no chances. Without a word, he unslung his rifle, cocked it and pulled the door open. The rifle barrel was pointed at the door, just in case. He was surprised to see the figure in the doorway. Even in the indistinct, flickering illumination of the lantern it was obvious he was looking at a girl.

'Who are you?' he blurted, and as the words left his lips he realized that he knew this person. It was Sela, Jaswant's girl.

'What are you doing here?' he stepped back, beckoning to her, 'Come on in...'

But she kept standing in the rain, her eyes also showing recognition of the soldier she faced.

'Did you come looking for Jaswant?' he asked.

She grasped the name he spoke, if nothing else, and nodded wordlessly. He put the safety catch on again, and slung the rifle across his back before gesturing with his hands, 'Gompa...he's gone to the Gompa...to look for...'

Before he could even complete the sentence, she was gone. He rushed out, as if to try and stop her. But she had disappeared into the gloom surrounding the log shelter.

He turned back into the hut, disappointed and not a little alarmed at the young girl's behaviour. Soon, time began to hang heavy on his thoughts, and he wished he and Jaswant hadn't split up. He didn't like being alone in this place. He was scared, he admitted to himself, and began to recite the Hanuman Chalisa.

He must have repeated the Lord's prayer about two dozen times, when the distinct sound of heavy footsteps fell on his ears. Again, he unslung his rifle and cocked it.

He needn't have worried, though. A couple of minutes later

he was staring at Jemadar Gabar Singh's grim countenance.

'What are you doing here, Gusain?' growled the Jemadar. The JCO looked deadbeat, as if he had been through hell. 'I saw the light flickering...in here...'

'Looking for you, Saabji. Jaswant and I. The Company Commander sent us out to look for you. But why are you alone, Saabji? Where...'

The JCO pointed, grimly, over his shoulder. 'We ran into a Chinese patrol, on the ridge outside town. We killed them all...but...' he shook his head, 'my men didn't make it, either.'

Gopal cast a glance around the shack, noticed an empty crate in a corner and dragged it up. 'Won't you sit down...you look exhausted, Saabji.'

'Where's Jaswant?'

Gopal explained how they had separated to better search for the Jemadar and his party. 'He should be along any moment now...I think.'

They waited close to an hour, in silence. Then, Gabar Singh glanced at his watch for the umpteenth time and got to his feet, 'Come...we can't wait here any longer.'

'But...Jaswant...'

'We'll look for him, instead of waiting for him to reach this place. You know the approximate direction he might have taken, don't you?'

'More or less...' nodded Gopal, as they left the log hut and plunged once more into the rain outside.

The two men had spent upwards of an hour trekking through the dark hillsides, steering clear of dwellings while keeping close to any available tracks, when suddenly Gopal exclaimed, 'Look! down there, Saabji! That looks like a hut. It's been crushed...maybe a landslide...'

'So? Anyone inside would be dead,' snapped the Jemadar. 'In any case, why would our man get into a place like that...'

'No, Saabji!' Gopal shone his light at the dilapidated basha, and an answering beam lit up, 'Look...there's someone there... alive!'

'Jaswant!' yelled Gopal, keeping his torch beam fixed on the hut, 'Jaswant...is that you? Jaswant...'

There was sudden activity inside the smashed hut. Then a figure emerged from the basha. It wasn't Jaswant, obviously. That much was evident in the light of their torches. But before the watching soldiers could react, the unknown had clambered and merged into the hillside.

'Wait, you!' Gabar Singh swung his sten gun around.

'No!' Gopal lunged across to swat the weapon off target, 'No, Saabji...'

'What the...' snarled the Jemadar, surprised at his colleague's reaction.

'Wait here, Saabji...cover me. I'll check,' Gopal was already scrambling down the barely discernible path and towards the hut. He found Jaswant, still groggy, with his shirt open and body smeared in slush. 'Jaswant! Wake up...quick! Get dressed!'

Before the Jemadar could make a move towards the hut, Gopal and Jaswant were struggling up the slippery, inclined path, their figures silhouetted against the darkness by the Jemadar's torch light.

'What were you doing there, Jaswant?' grated Gabar Singh. 'And who...who was that?'

Jaswant's eyes were downcast.

'What's the matter, Rifleman Jaswant Singh Rawat? Why don't you answer?'

It was Gopal who replied, 'That...was his wife, Saabji.'

'What the...' the Jemadar looked bewildered, 'What are you saying, Gopal? Wife...here? I don't understand. When... when did you get married, Jaswant?'

'A short while ago, Saabji,' explained Gopal, exchanging a quick glance with his best friend, 'He...was saying goodbye to her...'

'Hmph!' snorted Gabar Singh, hefting his Sten gun and marching away in the direction from where they had come. 'I'm glad we haven't all got our wives here. Can you imagine what would happen if all of us spent this time saying goodbye, with the enemy at the gates of Tawang?'

❦

For Sela, having the enemy at the gates seemed to be the perfect time to say goodbye, to the life she had lived all these years, carefree and selfish. She was now going to live for another, dedicate the remaining days of her life to helping him do what he was here to do—soldiering.

That at least was what she thought, as she left the town and marched for a while along the Tawang-Jang track, in the hope of tracking the retreating Indian soldiers. But Jaswant was not among the few stragglers that she did find. They were mostly Sikhs, plodding aimlessly through these unknown hills and valleys, themselves looking for some kind of succour. A few of them even asked the young girl whether she could help them find shelter. Some were badly hurt, with shrapnel injuries or bullet holes that had only stopped bleeding because there was no more blood left in their exhausted bodies to give. A couple of these men died at her feet, and she took time off her quest to hide their bodies under stones or hastily ripped vegetation. Although she knew this was none of her business, and that these Indian soldiers cared as little for her as did the Chinese in Tawang, Sela was now beginning to feel a strange kinship with the defeated men. They were Jaswant's comrades.

For food, she survived on the dry rations she found in the pouches or backpacks of some of these dead soldiers. It kept her from starvation.

'They took a few prisoners,' she heard at last from a Sikh. The words *'pakde gaye'* she had heard before and she presumed he was referring to his colleagues being captured by the Chinese. He smiled weakly, breathing his last in her arms. 'I... I am glad I didn't fall into their hands. Please don't... don't let them get my body, little girl...' Although she couldn't understand most of what he was saying, she could not help a wan smile. The dying soldier was himself not very much older than she. He might even have been her Jaswant, minus the beard and turban.

As she dragged the Sikh's body into a crevice in the rock and concealed it with stones and bushes, an idea began to take shape in Sela's mind. If there were indeed some Indian soldiers that had been taken prisoner... she decided then and there that she was going to give it a go. By then, it had become dark and had started to rain heavily. It rained all evening, and she had to wait with the dead soldier's body by her side. The gram and jaggery she found in the Sikh's pouches helped her keep hunger at bay. Soon, she fell asleep, exhausted.

When she woke up, it was dawn and the sky clear. It took her all day to trudge back to Tawang, in her present weakened state.

Once in the vicinity of the hamlet, she resisted the urge to return home. She was certain that if her father set eyes upon her again, he would tie her up to prevent her escaping. He might even give her away...to that scheming yak herder. With a heavy heart, because she missed her sister very much in this hour of crisis, Sela avoided the stone and bamboo dwelling that had been home to her for close to seventeen years, and pressed on in the direction of the town.

By now, Tawang was crawling with the Chinese. Because there were other Monpas—men and women—running errands for the victors, for a while Sela managed to escape detection. She even tried to speak to some of these natives, her own people, to find out about any Indian prisoners the Chinese might have taken. But most of the Monpas shied away from her questions, some eyeing her suspiciously, while others did not even look up from their chores.

Without the plumed yak skin cap that she now realized she had forgotten at home in her anxiety to leave, her dishevelled hair flew wildly about her ears and shoulders. Try as she might, Sela could not hide her comeliness from prying eyes. By and by, such lascivious glances settled upon the beautiful young teenager. Soon, a couple of soldiers fell into step with the fugitive Monpa girl, and before long two pairs of rough hands grasped her arms.

'So, are you looking for work, little Monpa girl?' the Chinese officer before whom the captive was presented had picked up a smattering of the dialect, as part of the PLA's preparation for the invasion. Senior Captain Xie also thought he had a way with women. This India-conqueror's plan had been to take a fresh flower to bed every night after his battalion stepped into Tawang. But as soon as he set eyes on this blossom, he determined that she was going to be the queen of his heart. His battle-hardened eyes had not seen so pretty a face in years. There was no telling how much longer this war was going to continue, or what fresh inroads his battalion might be called upon to make into enemy territory, in the eternal glory of the great Chairman Mao's resolve of teaching these stupid Indians a lesson. He might very well not find another such prize as this girl who now stood before him, with her eyes blazing away, bold and unafraid.

'Unhand me, you devils!' she hissed. 'When my Jaswant finds out he will stick his bayonet into your belly and tear you in half...'

'Jas...Jas...wan... What did you say?' The officer enjoyed taking spirited girls to bed. Now he laughed, mirthlessly, 'Who is this Jas...wan?'

The soldiers who held Sela immobilized between them also followed their officer's lead and guffawed, obediently.

'This champion of yours, girl... Is he a god? Or is he a soldier who will stick his knife in me...' Senior Captain Xie's eyes narrowed with suspicion, and he turned to his men, 'Go! Go look for this Jas...wan. Fools! What are you gaping at? Get out there and check... maybe she brought an Indian soldier along...'

The two soldiers trotted out of the room, their heels clomping on the wooden floor of the APO's office that was now the Chinese battalion headquarters.

'You are beautiful, and I would not wish to crush such a tender flower. But your arrogance must be stamped out, Monpa girl,' Xie said when they were alone in the room. He whipped off the leather belt that held his coat in place and started to thrash Sela with it. As she winced in agony he snarled, 'First, I will teach you that we are the masters. Then, you will see that a virile Chinese man is a far better lover than these spineless Indians who have run away from us like rabbits chased by wolves.'

Tears stung Sela's eyes as the heavy leather shred her

chemise, but she did not weep, or even let out a whimper of pain. She was not going to die, or give up, until she had set eyes once more upon her Jaswant.

When the Chinese officer was tired of beating her with his belt he tore off his coat and was unbuckling his trousers in a frenzy of lust when the door of the room burst open and one of the two soldiers entered again.

'What is it, you son of a whore?' yelled Xie, 'Can't you see I'm...'

The soldier hung his head in contrition, saying, 'Fresh orders from Headquarters, Senior Captain... Sir. The Indians are setting up their defensive position in Se La. We are to complete the Jang road in double quick time.'

'What the hell!' growled the officer at this unexpected impediment to his plans. Pulling up his trousers and buttoning his coat, he threw a threatening glance at Sela, who cowered in a corner. 'I'll be back to show you what a Chinese lover is capable of, Monpa girl. You...fools! Give her food and water... but don't let her out of your sight, understand?'

# 14

Noora, her father and Thabo stayed put inside the house for two days. The yak herder had arrived soon after Noora returned, and he did not go away on the pretext that he was loath to leave the old man and his daughter alone, in these dangerous times. As for Noora's father, there was nothing for him to go back to, in Tawang. With the Chinese taking over the entire area, there were now no Indian officials left in the APO's colony, and so there were to be no more meetings, not unless the Chinese overlords decided that they had any use for the Gam Budhas.

So now, the old man stayed home and tried to insinuate, through gestures and his demeanour, that Noora should not cold shoulder Thabo any more. The young *brokpa* had come to live with his prospective father-in-law and the daughter according to tradition, and if the war had not intervened Thabo and Sela, or even Noora, might very well have become man and wife.

The old man slept in the room upstairs, and let his daughter and son-in-law-to-be occupy the room below with its hearth, during the evenings and night. He even arranged a clean mattress for them by the fire, with a wide soft pillow that he had reserved for just such an occasion. He hoped the inviting warmth of the bed would help the young man and woman consummate their relationship and free him of the responsibility of at least one daughter.

But this was not to be. Although Thabo kept calling out to her in hoarse whispers all through the two nights, Noora kept resolutely to her own mattress across the fire, and did not even look at him. Her thoughts were elsewhere—with her missing sister.

When at last on the third morning Thabo roared in anger and frustration and started to tug at the straps of his luggage, pretending that he was going to leave the house, the old man asked, querulously, 'Have you two not been getting along, eh?'

Thabo grunted and looked away. Noora said, stoically, 'I am going out to look for my sister.'

'Fool of a girl! Do not throw your life away on account of her,' said the father, his voice heavy with grief.

Thabo picked remnants of breakfast from his teeth and said with satisfaction, 'She is probably dead. All the Monpas of Tawang work for the Chinese now, and the women who refused to bed with them have been raped and killed.'

A shudder moved Noora's frame at this, but she said, 'I am going to look for her... nevertheless...'

'Wait!' Thabo got to his feet, 'I'll go. I know some of the Chinese officers.'

He stomped out of the house. Noora and her father did not speak to one another all day, going about their chores in and around the dwelling as if the other did not exist.

When Thabo returned late in the day, he looked satisfied. In response to the old man's anxious gaze he nodded, 'Your other daughter is alive. The Chinese have her. They have not violated or killed her yet, because I requested them not to. But they want me to work for them and be their agent. I said I would do so, for Sela's sake. You see...?' he looked reproachfully at Noora, 'I am sacrificing everything for her sake. And you...you do not even share my bed when it is my right as your husband.'

'You are not yet my husband. Where is my sister?'

'She will be home safe, if I go back and tell the Chinese that I agree to their terms. And, they are running short of salt and churpi. I have to take some for the Chinese officers.'

'There is plenty in the house. Noora has been working hard, stocking up for the winter,' said the old man. 'As it is, we shall be fortunate if we manage to live through this season. Carry as much salt and milk fat as you want, son. Give it to those Chinese, but get my daughter back.'

Noora stood up, and touched the yak herder on the arm. In her eyes was a look of resignation, 'Just bring her back. Take what you want...from me...'

Thabo tried to smother an exultant look, 'I will go only in the morning. She is safe for the time being.'

'The Chinese officer...the Senior Captain...we are good friends now. He promised not to harm your sister,' he told Noora later that night, caressing her naked shoulder. The fire in the hearth was blazing with fresh, large logs that he had put in. 'You must relax.'

Noora was on the mattress with Thabo, the one that her father had prepared for them to be man and wife. She did not resist when the man took off her chemise and pulled her into his arms. She was quiet while he had his way with her, grunting and groaning like one of the yaks that he had been rearing so assiduously, all his life.

She mumbled, almost distractedly, 'Let Sela go...to the man she loves...'

When he was spent and snoring loudly by her side, Noora remained awake. She thought of her sister and prayed Sela was safe. She also prayed for Jaswant, that he would return after the war to his own village in mountains thousands of miles away from this spot.

Better to be the wife of this herder whom she would never love, than to lose her honour to those dreadful, unwelcome Chinese. They were, after all, mortal enemies of her Jaswant. Yes, she knew at last the name of the man she loved, and that the Garhwali Rifleman named Jaswant would never ever belong to her as he would to her sister. He had made love to her only because he mistook her for Sela. Yet, it was a fact that she had possessed his love for one brief, fleeting moment. That was enough, the young woman reckoned, for the brief life that remained to her. For Noora had no doubt, this gloomy evening, that after the Chinese hordes had swept over the mountain spurs and into the valleys of her childhood, nothing would remain of her, or her loved ones.

She only wished she could make it up to her sister, in some manner.

Jaswant had no hope that he would survive the war, or return to Dehradun to see his family, again. In fact, none of the soldiers of 'A' Company harboured such ambitions, any longer. They knew that they had been left behind at Jang as cannon fodder while 62 Brigade consolidated its positions at Se La Pass.

No one entertained any illusions regarding the course the war was going to take. Having overrun Tawang, the Chinese were quiet. The few Chinese, arriving in the vicinity of Nuranang, were camped north of the Tawang Chu. The river now separated the Indians and the Chinese. 'C' Company of 4 Garhwal waited south of the river, waiting for orders to demolish the bridge, should the Chinese try to cross.

Over the next few days, a battalion of Chinese gathered on the ridges overlooking the Nuranang valley. Their artillery had the drop on the Indians. The Garhwalis were able to do little when the Chinese shelled them, exposed as they were in the valley below, near Bridge 4. A few men died because of the Chinese pounding, and the Garhwalis were relieved when their CO decided that the battalion should withdraw to the open ground four miles downstream of Jang, near the Bridge 3. The battalion's stores and kitchens were set up here, as were the transport units.

A couple of the cooks had been killed in the shelling, and Jaswant was one of the jawans detailed to help in the kitchen. He was frustrated, because this restricted his movements, just when he was hoping he might be in one of the patrols tasked to go out in the direction of the Tawang Chu, for keeping tabs on the Chinese.

'Don't worry. All that cooking you did for your employers in Dehradun will come in handy here,' Gopal consoled him, while he himself prepared to leave camp as part of a recce patrol. Noticing his friend's desperate glance, he winked, saying in a hoarse whisper, 'Trust me, I'll keep an eye out for her. I promise. You just make sure the rotis taste...like my mother's, eh?'

Despite his anguish, Jaswant could not help smiling at his friend. The news was that although there had been some casualties among the civilians of Tawang, many among the town's population had managed to leave their homes before the Chinese had entered, and had escaped to presumably safer areas, in the nearby villages or even south towards Assam.

The sounds of blasting was now a constant refrain in the air. The Garhwalis knew the Chinese were at it again, building roads through their conquered areas so they might bring forward the bulk of their infantry and heavy weapons and equipment.

The wireless crackled continuously. Messages flew back and forth between 'A' Company Commander and Battalion Headquarters. Rations were running low in the Quartermaster's stores, and the skills Jaswant had acquired through his teens, in making do with available groceries to create the best possible food, now came in handy. The bunkers and the trenches frequently rang with cries of 'Wah! Wah!' as Jaswant's culinary abilities found almost daily application. But the rifleman himself was far from content. He waited anxiously for Gopal Gusain's patrol to return.

Gopal had this to say when he marched into the makeshift battalion kitchen on the open ground, without even pausing to change out of his dirt caked uniform and boots, 'The Chinese are gathering in great numbers. If the speed of their road building is any indication, they will come for us, sooner rather than later. I hope you have been feeding our comrades well, Jaswant. God only knows if any of us will live to see another Diwali. These damned Chinese....don't they celebrate any festivals? They're perpetually busy, like ants, crawling all over the place, blasting rock and levelling roads. Wonder what they're made of... slave drivers! Slaves...yes, that reminds me,' he added, noticing his friend's desperate, impatient expression, 'We did see some girls... young Monpa girls, they looked like. The Chinese seem to be using them to fulfil all their requirements... I mean...no, I don't...but...'

Jaswant dropped his ladle and lunged toward his friend, gripping him by a shoulder, 'Did you...did you...' he swallowed, unable to finish the question.

Gopal took his friend by the chin, and smiled, 'No, Jaswant. She wasn't among them. They have not taken her…alive…I hope so.'

'I must go to her!' Jaswant said through gritted teeth. 'I… I have to find her, Gopal. I must find her before something… anything happens to her. Just let me feel her tender gaze once more…then I am quite willing to die.'

'But how will you go out there, buddy? You can't return to Tawang, even presuming that the Company Commander will let you out of this kitchen. The town is too dangerous, right now. To cross that river is certain death. The Chinese control everything on that side.'

'If I stay…that will be death, too.'

As if in response to the soldiers' angst came this pronouncement from the newly appointed Brigade Commander, on his first visit to the battalion since assuming command of 62 Brigade, 'It is not that the Army High Command doubts your valour, or the ability of this battalion to give a good account of itself. But there are higher objectives, goals that our superiors can see, with their view from the top. We, down here, can only see a few kilometres in front of us or behind, even with our binoculars. But the Generals at Headquarters, and our great leaders in Delhi, have a vision for the nation's future. All our actions must correspond to that vision…'

'Does that mean we will never see action, Sir? Only keep hopping from place to place until our canvas shoes are completely worn out and our meagre rations gone?'

The Brigadier's eyes sought the soldier who had dared to speak, interrupting his address to the Officers, JCOs and ORs of 4 Garhwal Rifles.

'Who was that?' snarled a Major, the Brigade Intelligence Officer. 'How dare you…'

Rifleman Jaswant Singh Rawat jumped to his feet, presenting arms in salute.

The Brigadier said, 'Let him speak, Major. Well, what is it you were saying, son? Action…so you want to see action? You will, boy. The Indian Army is going to show what stuff we are made of, here in Nuranang and at Se La. We shall teach those Chinese a lesson they will never forget. And, as for your canvas shoes and poor rations, be grateful for what you have. There are people in our country who walk barefoot and do without one square meal a day…' The Commander's eyes raked the gathering of jawans, seated in neat, symmetrical rows with their .303 single shot rifles resting across their knees, 'Any more questions?'

'That Jaswant!' muttered Jemadar Gabar Singh to the Subedar standing closest to him. 'He'll get us all into hot water with the bosses…and himself court-martialled for insubordination. The fool!'

'But he has a point,' Subedar Udai Singh mumbled in reply, 'We could have given a good account of ourselves back there in Tawang. All that preparation and waiting…for nothing! At the first sign of trouble, we turn tail and run…'

A few minutes later, the Brigadier's jeep roared away up the road to Se La, where most of 62 Brigade was encamped, preparing to make the stand that the officer had been telling them about.

4 Garhwal Rifles would remain at Jang, holding positions and delaying the expected Chinese advance across the Tawang Chu via Bridge No 4. 'A' Company had the responsibility of guarding the approach beyond the bridge, and blowing it up

when the Chinese got too close.

However, the invaders appeared in no hurry to get a move on. The Indian intelligence reported that the Chinese, having accomplished their first objective of taking Tawang, would now spend some time consolidating their positions in and around the town. But they would press home their advantage, without doubt. And, every soldier in 62 Brigade was ready to join battle. For the remnants of the Gurkhas, Grenadiers and Sikhs, it could mean another chance to have a go at the Chinese, to exact some measure of retribution for the hammering they got in Dhola. They had fought bravely and well, but there is no gainsaying defeat.

As for the Garhwalis, they could only hope their turn would come, sooner rather than later. Meantime, they set about the inevitable trench-digging and bunker building, even as the whining icy winds told them the cold weather would come upon them before the Chinese did, probably an enemy more to be feared than the men from across the border.

To camouflage their apprehensions, the soldiers talked incessantly, to each other if not to the walls of their bunkers. 'Here we are...listening to the whining of these hostile winds and preparing for the noise of mortar shells, and there at home preparations would be on for Diwali and the happy sounds of firecrackers...'

'Yes. Mother must be preparing laddoos and jalebis. Maybe, when she feeds my younger brother, she will be reminded of my open mouth, too.'

'What can I say of the roat and urad ki pakori that mother prepares!' Negi's memories transported him back home, 'Wah wah! No sooner would I open my mouth to eat than she would pop one between my jaws. I can hear her say, 'at least move your limbs when you have to eat. How long do you expect me to feed you like a child?' I am quite sure father has already been to Sadar Bazaar, looking for firecrackers at bargain prices. We were the family that created the most noise with crackers during Diwali, in our mohalla.'

Naik Ranjit Singh, on the other hand, was glum, 'My… father…he detested the noise and smell of crackers. Ours would always be the quietest house in the neighbourhood. But not this time!' the veteran's bleak eyes sparkled for a moment, 'No… not this Diwali. My younger sister warned him. There will be noise and colour this Diwali. "We now have a pretty sister-in-law to celebrate with, don't we?" she asked. "My bhaiya and my bhabhi…this will be their first Diwali together," she said. "So we're going to make it special, make as much noise as we can, Papa…"' Jaspal had been visiting his family, when the emergency had been declared, and all leaves had been cancelled. In a trice, the newlywed found himself on the North-East Frontier. The guests had probably not even left his house before he had to leave behind his bride and come up here to this desolation. He shrugged, sighing and gesturing to his mates, 'Well, fellows… it looks like the noise is going to be more than we bargained for, after all.'

For once, Jaswant sat quiet and morose, listening to this banter. Negi noticed the young jawan's distraction and chuckled, 'Hey, look at Jaswant! He doesn't seem to be enjoying his Diwali here. What is it, Jaswant? Missing your family?'

'Family?' Gopal Gusain asked, on his friend's behalf. 'Everyone celebrates Diwali at home…but not our hero…'

'Why? Did he have a girlfriend there, too?'

Jaswant looked darkly at the one who made this insinuation, but held his peace.

Gopal glanced at his crony. 'He only went home for the puja on Diwali.'

'Why…why would he do that?' urged Negi.

'He was mostly with Manoj Bhaiya.'

'Manoj Bhaiya?'

'Yes, Manoj is the son of a Colonel…back in Dehradun. Diwali at their place was always so glittering and grand. Not like in our simple homes…'

'How do you know, Gopal?'

'I went along, once. That is how I know. The Colonel's family got boxes of sweets, and piles of dry fruits. And what grand clothes every one of them purchased for Diwali! There was so much coming, going…and parties. The Colonel's wife would wear new ornaments. And Uncle, the Colonel, would treat his guests out of his bottles of expensive liquor. How grand their Diwali celebrations used to be! Our Jaswant would always say… "One day, when I become an officer…"'

'Officer?' someone chuckled. 'But of course. If any one of us is officer material, it is our Jaswant. But first, we have to get out of this alive, eh?'

'Listen to a rifleman's dreams,' another laughed aloud. 'We are all going to die!'

'Shut up, you fools!' snarled Subedar Udai Singh, 'Let's not have that kind of talk at this time. And I quite agree…about Jaswant. He will make a fine officer one day.'

'What about you, Subedar Saab? Don't you want to be Honorary Captain before you retire? That's the least you can do for your family…'

'Of course, I do. But, you fellows don't have any idea of what we are facing here, do you? I spoke with some of the Sikhs who returned from Dhola sector, as they were passing through

Tawang. "Hindi-Chini Bhai Bhai", my foot! Those Chinese... they have been planning this...for years. And now they're coming at us with everything they've got. If we want to beat them, each one of us will have to kill a hundred of them.'

'"*Sawaa lakh naal ek ladawaan*... each one of my braves shall be equal to one hundred thousand of the enemy..." Isn't that what Guru Gobind told his Sikhs?'

'Right. If the Sikhs can do it, we Garhwalis can do it better!' Trilok Singh Negi stood up and shook his rifle, 'Let our two hands be like the eight arms of the Mother Goddess. May the determination in our eyes be like Bhawani's fiery, all-consuming glare,' he roared.

'You will make a good poet. Sit down, Negi!' snapped the Subedar. 'This is no time for heroics. We must remain calm if we are to defeat the Chinese. They are superior in every way...uniforms, equipment, ammunition, transport and communication. And, don't take them for cowards. Remember, they drove the Japanese from their land, a few years ago. They made great sacrifices, too. What do we have that they don't?'

There was sudden silence inside the bunker. Each member of that Garhwali platoon looked at one another, waiting for someone else to speak.

By and by, Jaswant Singh Rawat, raised out of stupor by this challenge, gave voice to their feelings, 'We are defending our homes. We have the love of our mothers, our sisters and our beloveds, whom we must protect from these invaders. That, alone, should be enough. I, for one, will not leave this place alive, unless I have killed every one of the enemy...or until they retreat. I swear...'

'Tell that to the higher ups,' Gopal dug an elbow into his friend's ribs, 'Who will make them understand? As for you, my childhood friend, I don't want you to face a court martial on account of a Monpa girl. So keep your mouth shut and your eyes open, Jaswant.'

# 15

When three days passed without Thabo making good his promise to bring Sela back home, Noora began to lose hope of ever seeing her sister again. She would spend the day going through her chores about the house like an automaton.

Already shattered by the seeming loss of one daughter, the old man could bear Noora's distress no more. He held his child close and wept, saying, 'We have each other, my little one. This storm too shall pass. You must make a new life with Thabo. He may only be a yak herder, but he is wealthy and he has influence with the Chinese. My bones will wither away soon. Thabo will take good care of you…'

She looked dully at her father. When the herder forced himself upon her every night, she barely stirred, lying with glazed eyes and a faint prayer.

She resolved then, that as soon as the opportunity offered she would leave this house and go out to look for Jaswant. He was somewhere out there in the wilderness, preparing for another battle. She understood her Jaswant. He would stand and fight.

But for now, she could not abandon the old man. Noora

could not forget the years that her father had spent with his two little girls, tending to their every need after their mother died of a fever. How was she to ignore the nights he stayed awake when one of them burned with fever, the times he would go frantic with worry when the girls quarrelled and he tried to make peace between them.

Opportunity came knocking when Thabo decided that he would go into the hills to bring down a couple of his yaks. His business partner had run away with the other escaping Monpas, and Thabo was afraid that his herd might be dispersed if he did not attend promptly to them. He was also planning to gift two animals to the Chinese officer, who was proving difficult. Having promised earlier to release the pretty Monpa girl in exchange for two sacks of salt and some milk fat, the Senior Captain, according to the two soldiers who were serving as the conduit between the officer and Thabo, now wanted two whole yaks, before he could consider releasing such a good-looking woman.

The herder would be gone at least one whole day, Noora knew. She saw him whispering in her father's ears, and from time to time Thabo's eyes would flit towards Noora, although she assumed an indifferent demeanour.

'Now we are running out of salt and maize flour, father,' she went up to the old man when they were alone in the house again. His bleary eyes barely glanced at her, in them a faraway look, as if he cared no more about the goings on in this hate-weary world. 'I will go and check at Rincin's house. I am aware that the family have left, but I do know where they keep a second key hidden. Maybe Rincin's family have not carried away all their provisions. If I can find some maize flour and salt… there is no knowing whether we will get another opportunity…

before the fighting starts again… Then, it will be impossible to go…if we are all still alive…'

The old man nodded almost by reflex, and even got up from his chair to accompany his daughter to the door of their home. He stood in the doorway for a long while after the young girl's figure had disappeared in the morning mist, his right hand raised and waving goodbye.

Noora found the key as presumed. There were indeed some surplus stores in Rincin's house, which the family had left behind when they fled Tawang. Entering the kitchen, Noora started to prepare food. When she thought she had done enough, she packed the food in containers and the liquor in bamboo *pallangs*. Stuffing the tiffin boxes and pallangs carefully into a haversack, she left the house and stepped on to the Jang road.

She knew the terrain well. All the mithun and goat tracks in and around Tawang were etched in her mind. But because she had to keep off the main road, travel was not going to be easy, and would take her many more hours. She might even have to spend a couple of nights camping out in the wild. The ravines and jungles held no terrors for Noora, or even the dark, but she was afraid of being discovered by the Chinese. She did not fear for herself. But she did not wish to be caught before she had attained her objective.

When Noora had travelled thus for two days, keeping herself alert by resting frequently and eating frugally of the provisions that she carried, she appeared to be no nearer to achieving her goal than she had been two days ago when she set out.

The invaders, it seemed, were everywhere. The Chinese soldiers were in their blue caps and the camp follower slaves in blue dresses—like an army of blue ants. It looked like they were repairing the road towards Jang. There were now too many Chinese soldiers and Monpa coolies spread all along the main track, making it impossible for her to hazard an approach.

By and by, on the third morning she found herself close to the river that cut the Jang road. She would have to cross the Nuranang Chu if she wanted to follow the Garhwalis. Given the current state of affairs, that was impossible. The Chinese had their camps spread out all along the river on either side of the bridge close to Jang. The river was a torrent on this stretch, and she knew that she had no hope of crossing that bridge without being sighted.

Noora waited one more day among some wooded slopes close to the bridge, and kept herself alive by consuming the food and liquor she had carried with her. By and by, this was also on the point of running out, and she realized that she had better go back to the house if she was to have any chance of survival. She would have to return to the Jang Bridge later, but only after the Chinese had crossed over and had moved further down the road.

So, with a heavy heart and a much lighter haversack, she started back in the direction of Tawang. She was not going back home, that much was certain. Thabo would have returned with his yaks from his farm in the hills by now, and he would be enraged to find that Noora had left without his permission. He was not going to offer her another such opportunity if he could help it, she realized, and so decided to stay put at Rincin's house until the time was ripe for one more sortie in the direction of the Jang Bridge.

Thabo was depressed. He was no nearer his goal of possessing Sela. Even after delivering the two yaks to the Senior Captain, he was made to wait almost interminably and then fobbed off with the excuse that the officer had to visit his superior and would only consider releasing the Monpa girl when he returned.

Now Noora also was gone. The incensed yak herder scolded the girls' father, holding him responsible for this state of affairs. He even threatened to bring the Chinese here, and they would teach everyone a lesson. By and by, the herder realized that his words were making no discernible impression upon the old man.

Frustrated, the bile rising in him, Thabo decided that drastic action was called for. At that, he stomped out of the house again, determined to join issue with the Chinese. He was not going to stand for this nonsense any longer.

But as the sturdy, young man, who was now a familiar figure for the Chinese entrenched in Tawang, marched back to the office of the Senior Captain, he could not help noticing that the invaders seemed to be extremely busy with preparations. Perhaps another offensive was in the works. The town was crawling with armed men. Seeing the soldiers' bleak eyes and their set jaws, the herder decided that it might not be such a good idea to quarrel with the Chinese after all. If they were preparing to move out, the Chinese might have no use for him or his services, for much longer. In that event, they might need little excuse to make him also a prisoner or a slave, or even to put a bullet through his head.

The thought was like cold water poured over his head, and the herder's plodding brain now began to try to figure out another way to solve his problem. Just as he reached Xie's office, the penny dropped. He knew what he must do.

'I have an offer for you, Sir,' said Thabo when the two guards had reluctantly ushered him into the presence of their superior.

Senior Captain Xie looked distastefully at the herder. He

wished he could get rid of this smelly yak herder who kept bothering him about the Monpa girl. Xie had decided that the girl was going to be his mistress. He would take her back home after the war was over. And no one was going to stop him from doing that, not even the Colonel of his regiment.

'Haven't my men told you? We do not need any more meat or milk fat. And the regiment is moving. So, you needn't come here again.'

'I...I only came because I have some...some valuable information,' Thabo said, trying to sound calm, unctuous. 'I thought anything of value... I must tell your Excellency about it first...'

'Oh?' the officer looked suspiciously at the Monpa. 'What is it? You'd better not waste my time, eh?'

'Shall we take him outside and shoot him, Sir?' asked one of the soldiers, helpfully, and Thabo shuddered.

'Shut up, you fool!' Xie glared at his subordinate, 'Can't you see I'm talking to the man? You...what were you saying?'

'There...there is another girl. She...that girl in your custody...she has a sister, Sir. Even more beautiful than her.'

'So?'

'I...I could bring her here, Sir. If your honour agrees, I will go this instant. Then, maybe...maybe...'

Xie had quite made up his mind about his fair prisoner. But he still wanted to see what this fool of a herder had to offer. There was no harm in having two good-looking mistresses. And if they were sisters, so much the better. After all, had the great Chairman himself not set such a sterling example for all Chinese with his bevy of women? The Senior Captain had no doubt that, if he cultivated these civilized habits, he would eventually rise high in the echelons of the People's Liberation

Army, and one day become part of the ruling clique of the People's Republic of China. How he looked forward to that day, and the confrontation he was going to have with that stuck-up fool of a Colonel, who sat in his comfortable office and thought he knew everything about fighting a war!

The officer sighed, and fixed his baleful gaze upon the Monpa. 'I must see her first, before I decide. So go and do your duty for the conquerors of Tawang. And don't return until you have the girl, or it will go hard with you.'

When the yak herder had gone, Xie told his guards, 'Bring the girl some decent clothes. I do not want her to look like a beggar of a Monpa. She now belongs to a Senior Captain of the People's Liberation Army. She must look the part—stylish and wealthy. And remember...if anyone dares lay a finger on her...she is only a bud now, soon to be the flower of Xie's household.'

'But...but how can we...we...carry her along when the regiment marches, Sir? If the Colonel hears of this...he...the CO is a disciplinarian, Sir. If he hears...'

'If that happens Senior Captain Xie will have to employ two new guards, eh?' the officer's lips parted in a snarl, and the soldiers quaked in their boots. 'So...you'd better make sure no one hears about the bud in the Senior Captain's garden. Is that clear?'

# 16

When Noora woke up in the morning, it seemed to her that she might have slept through an entire day and night. But there was no time for idle speculation. She now heard a loud, grinding sound, as of a great mass moving, remorselessly. Startled, she peeked through holes in the wall of the house, and saw a vast concourse of people and machines proceeding in the direction of Jang. The Chinese Army!

She hastily picked up the provisions that she had kept packed and ready in the haversack in a corner of Rincin's house, and slipped out through a window facing away from the main road.

It was just as well she did, for she had only put a few metres between herself and the house when a gun boomed and the wood, bamboo and stone house exploded like a petulant child's toy. The Chinese were on the road, infantry and artillery pushing inexorably in the direction of Se La Pass. It appeared that the invaders wanted to leave no stone or stick standing in their wake for the Indians to come back to, if that were conceivable.

She hid for a while, and just as the tail of the triumphant army passed her by, consisting of trucks and pack animals carrying the army's stores, accompanied by Tibetan and

Monpa slaves, she smuggled herself into the procession. No one appeared to notice or care about the addition of one solitary Monpa girl to that moving throng.

That the Chinese were planning to continue the assault and move in the direction of Se La Pass, she was now certain. Whatever happened, in the confusion of battle or afterwards, she would find an opportunity to cross that Bridge on the Tawang Chu, which she had been unable to negotiate upon her earlier attempt.

She saw a glimmer of hope when the regiment halted. Ducking into a gully leading off the main road, she almost stumbled and fell over a figure lying sprawled in the bushes. Struggling to her feet she was on the point of hurrying away when a thought occurred, and she paused. The body was strangely still. Noora bent, examined the blue clad figure. It was a Tibetan slave, probably shot by the Chinese. Quickly then, Noora stripped the blue uniform gown off the corpse and wore it over her chemise.

A couple of minutes later, Noora was in the thick of the Chinese camp, and busy obeying the commands thrown at her by the overseers, for whom she was just another slave. Sometimes she was fetching water, at other times cleaning tents. She was wearing an oversized felt hat with yak's hair fringes, which she had found in Rincin's house. It looked and smelt like the one belonging to Thabo the herder, but it helped to obscure most of her face from prying eyes. This and the bedraggled blue uniform of the unfortunate Tibetan woman made her look like a middle-aged worker rather than the young, pretty daughter of a Gam Budha of Tawang.

In any case, the Chinese were too busy at the moment making preparations for their next assault upon Indian positions across the river, to have any time for the slaves, even the attractive ones among them.

Noora's errands took her as far as the bridge. On her way back after supplying water to the soldiers who were setting up the artillery or taking positions along the riverfront, she contrived to lose her way without being noticed by any of her slave companions, and blended into the forest close to the river's bank. She climbed the rock, slowly and with a quiet desperation, until she reached a vantage point from where she could see across the river.

The Indians were there, on the open ground not very far from the river. She even caught sunlight glinting off rifle barrels or the polish of guns placed close to the Indian entrenchments. Unfortunately, there was no way she could make out whether those Indians belonged to Jaswant's battalion. They were too far away.

She returned to the Chinese camp late in the evening, dodging sentries so that no one might ask uncomfortable questions about a lone Tibetan woman walking through the Chinese positions. After a while, the Chinese guns began to boom. Maybe the attack had begun. Perhaps they were trying to cross the river. She had no way of knowing; curiosity might prove fatal at this juncture. So, as night fell, Noora curled up between a pair of rocks, hugging her haversack tightly. No one, she surmised, would pay any attention to her now that the battle was imminent.

When she woke suddenly from an exhausted slumber, all was still. But her faculties understood that the night was at an end. Another dawn, laden with fear and suspicion and hope, was within hailing distance. Even before the first tongues of light licked the sky, though, guns began to thunder. From the location of the sounds, she reckoned that the Chinese artillery had opened up. Soon there was a rattle of small arms fire, followed by distant war cries.

She lay awake, with her eyes open while her senses tried to ignore this dance of death, being played out in the distance.

Then, as abruptly as it had begun, the fighting stopped and a profound silence reigned in the hills. Activity in the camp roused her again, as she was drifting off to sleep, her bones weary from the previous day's march.

Noora was still wondering whether she should get up on her feet when something hard and sharp stabbed into her side, doubling her up in momentary agony. A gruff voice followed the rude awakening, 'On your feet, woman! Enough rest for you.' A Chinese sentry's bayonet was prodding her in the ribs.

Touching her side gingerly, she struggled to her feet. Fortunately, the thick fabric of the blue uniform over her chemise had protected her skin from the razor-sharp steel. She nodded wordlessly, bowing her head in submission, and leaned over to pick up her haversack.

'Hey! Slave…leave your sack be. You're wanted there… see that? By that tent. There's food kept there. Pick it up and carry it into the tent. Hurry… go quickly before the Senior Captain has you shot for disobedience…' and the sentry watched Noora hurrying off toward the tent he had indicated.

❦

'The Chinese appear to have gone to sleep,' announced Subedar Jatan Singh, saluting his Company Commander. 'There is no activity on their side, Shriman. Our patrol went as far as they could penetrate, close to the river. There was no firing from the enemy's side… nothing at all.'

2nd Lt Tandon was deep in thought for a while, before shaking his head. 'It's the calm...before the storm. They are up to something. Get on that radio, Subedar Saab...crank it up and get HQ. We must warn Brigade at Se La to be ready.'

'We shan't let the Chinese get to Se La Pass, Saabji.'

'We're outnumbered, Jatan Singh. There is at least one regiment of the Chinese facing us, across this river.'

'In that case, Saabji... we will sell our lives dearly.' The JCO clicked his heels and went into the radio shack.

Behind him, the 2nd Lieutenant looked out over the lowering black mountains of the evening, 'This is it...the big one...'

In one of the bunkers overlooking Bridge 4, Trilok Singh Negi licked the dried glue lining the edges of the inland letter he had just filled with his neat, diligently wrought handwriting, before folding it neatly.

'Hey, where are you going to post that letter of yours, Negi?' Gopal Gusain was chuckling, leaning on his .303 Lee Enfield. 'I don't suppose there will be any mail van going out of Battalion HQ for some time to come.'

Negi met his gaze and sighed. Then he stretched his right hand out, holding the closed inland letter. 'I was going to give it to you. Here...keep this safe. If anything happens to me, this is for my wife...my family. At least, they will know that I died fighting...a Garhwali to the end.'

Gopal tucked the letter carefully into his ammunition pouch and smiled. 'You bet I'll give it to them...old friend. Don't worry.'

'Aren't you going to leave...a letter...?' asked Negi, as he peered down his rifle barrel before sliding a ramrod down the aperture. 'Something for them to remember you by...'

'I won't die,' Gopal shrugged.

'How do you know?'

'I...just know...'

Jaswant ducked into the bunker at that moment, saying, 'He's right, you know? He's immortal.'

'You're back!' Lance Naik Negi smiled at Jaswant. 'Immortal? What do you mean?'

'Don't you know? The soul...is eternal. It cannot be cut by weapons nor burned by fire. It is impervious to water and the wind...everlasting. I don't say that...the Bhagavad Gita does.'

'Try telling that to those Chinese waiting outside, eh?' Gopal laughed, nodding to Negi, 'This Jaswant is a deep one, isn't he? Here he is, trying to escape from his kitchen, with his hands still wreathed in chapati dough...and he speaks of immortality... eh...heh?'

'Give me my rifle,' said Jaswant, 'I'm through with cooking. The Quatermaster found a Sikh who lost his trigger finger... the poor chap is better off in the kitchen, they decided, and let me go. How's that for a lucky break?'

'Just you wait until those blue ants start attacking, and you will wish you were back in your kitchen...' Negi looked grim.

'Don't you want to finish your letter, Jaswant?' enquired Gopal, 'With that pen the Lieutenant Saab gifted you?'

'Yes, Jaswant...maybe it's time to say our goodbyes. Don't leave anything pending. You never know...' As if corroborating Negi's words, they heard distant thunder. 'There you are! Chinese artillery. Look to your weapons, men. On the double. We'll teach them a lesson, this time...that's for sure.'

'A' Company was ideally located to bear the brunt of any Chinese attack across the Tawang Chu. Even if they crossed Bridge 4, the attackers would have to overrun 'A' Company's positions on the right bank of the Nuranang chu, before gaining access to Bridge 3. The route southeast, towards Se La, lay across this bridge, on the left bank of the river.

Subedar Udai Singh Rawat and his platoon would be first in the line of fire.

'No one sleeps tonight,' said the platoon commander as he went from bunker to bunker checking on his men, quite unnecessarily as it turned out, because no one was going to be able to rest that evening. The soldiers' eyes watered with the strain of trying to pierce the darkness, and occasionally their limbs faltered in the steady rhythm of night patrol. Still, they kept awake, knowing the attack was going to come.

For Noora and Sela's father, life appeared to have come to a standstill. Yet, he marvelled that he continued to live, without a purpose. He recalled vaguely having experienced just such a feeling when his wife died, many years ago. But that time was different, because as it turned out his two little girls had given meaning to his life, a direction for his efforts as a parent. As he watched Noora and Sela grow from knee height to strapping young maidens, he was glad he had not followed his first impulse at the death of his wife, to follow her into the afterlife. His daughters had become the support of his youth and his middle age. The girls filled his stomach and his senses with their affection, and they were the song that uplifted his soul in every crisis.

Now the girls, too, were gone. First Sela…chasing her dream lover, and now Noora, he knew not where. The Gam Budha wished he had the courage to leave this house and go looking for them among the mountains and meadows. But he had not the vigour, nor the will.

That was how Thabo found the old man when he returned to the house. The girls' father sat with chin sunk upon his chest, his fingers drumming meaningless patterns across his arthritic knees.

'You must tell me where Noora is gone, old man,' the herder pressed. Even Thabo was not himself anymore. The earlier self-assurance was gone from his voice, 'Sela… I don't know what…will happen to her. But Noora…maybe we can still…'

The old man shook his head, muttering almost inaudibly. Grabbing his shoulders Thabo shook him, 'Speak, Sela's father, speak! I might still be able to save Noora. Remember that she is now *my* woman. I have lain with her these past days. Where… where is she gone? Where?'

The old man looked dully at his inquisitor for a moment, and then nodded. 'Rincin…try Rincin's house. She said…Noora said…millet dough and salt…we need…provisions…'

Thabo left, and soon discovered the pile of crushed bamboo and rubble that had been Rincin's house. Nothing could have survived that explosion. He scoured the embers of the wreck. Even in the remains of devastation like this, human remains would be distinguishable, he thought. Besides, he reasoned, if Noora had come here to collect supplies, and had not got back home, that meant she was headed elsewhere with the goods. Where could she have gone, in these circumstances, with Tawang in the grip of the Chinese, who were advancing ever eastward, obviously intending to sweep through Se La Pass and down to Bomdi La?

Then a thought crossed his mind. The herder recalled Noora's words to him, 'Take me for wife. Let Sela go to the man she loves…'

Had Noora, instead, gone to that man…the Indian…that

soldier whom he had hated at first sight, who had come between the yak herder and his promised bride, Sela?

At first, it seemed preposterous. But the longer he dwelt upon the possibility, the more did it seem probable that he was right. If so, had Noora followed the retreating Indians in the direction of Se La Pass?

Thabo had no illusions about his situation. If he caught up with the Chinese regiment, there was no certainty that the invaders would treat him with any consideration, now that they did not require his services anymore. As the days passed, the Senior Captain had clearly become more and more reluctant to unhand his prize catch, the beautiful Monpa girl. He might not take kindly to Thabo returning to claim Sela. If only the herder could trace Noora, and bring her before Xie—that might, just might change the officer's view.

Having determined upon one last throw of the dice, the herder mounted his mule and trotted off in the wake of the Chinese Army. The regiment and its supply train of animals and slaves had at least a day's lead on him. Thabo flogged his mule mercilessly until the beast foamed at the mouth. Still he pushed, not resting, determined to find Noora before anything happened to her and he lost his only hope of getting his Sela out of the clutches of the Chinese.

# 17

Senior Captain Xie was angry and frustrated. He was angry because the Colonel had questioned his leadership of the battalion. The Commanding Officer, if reports from headquarters were to be believed, was blaming Xie for the delay in crossing Bridge 4 and the present difficulties in breaching the defences of the Indians at Nuranang.

The Senior Captain was frustrated at the obduracy of his opponents. He had expected to find little resistance once the bridge across the Tawang Chu was crossed, and the road completed. However, even after throwing in his finest units against the Garhwalis, who were occupying the Nuranang valley, there had been little progress over the past two days.

His aggravation became more pronounced at the fact that he was unable to pay any attention to what he considered his most valuable conquest of this war—the Monpa girl. Raping a woman was easy for a vanquisher. But persuading the defeated—and more so when it is a desirable woman—to succumb to his overwhelming charms, is the dream of every conqueror. Xie had no doubt that he would win her over, if only he could spend a few, peaceful hours with his fair captive, undisturbed by the compulsions of war. Sadly, that was not to be. The Colonel, it seemed, was only waiting for the Senior Captain to put one step wrong so that he could send an adverse report to Beijing about the reasons for the delay in the PLA's imperious march to Bomdi La, in pursuit of the cowardly Indians.

Xie had become so overwrought by the state of affairs, that he shot the loyal Tibetan slave who had been part of his entourage from the beginning of this campaign. The unfortunate woman made the mistake of interrupting when the Senior Captain was in the tent allotted to his special prisoner. He had been hoping to impress upon the Monpa girl from Tawang the fact that there was no escape. He was becoming impatient with her tantrums. He was also running out of time, what with the ongoing battle, and the ever-present danger of any gossip about his passion for this woman reaching the ears of his superiors at military headquarters, or even Beijing.

The officer had been trying to take Sela in his arms, after slapping her a few times, when the Tibetan woman entered without warning. She was only bringing the liquor that he had called for. But, incensed as he already was by Sela's indifference, Xie flew into a rage at the interruption. Snatching up his pistol, he emptied the magazine at the slave.

'That is going to be your fate too, girl!' he barked at Sela, who sat hunched on the cot inside the tent, her face turned away from her tormentor. 'I will return when I've taken care of those…Gar…Garwaalis…those Garwaalis beyond the bridge. I will crush them! So shall I crush you, too, my reluctant flower, if you don't change your ways…'

As the officer stamped out of the tent, kicking the dead Tibetan's body, which lay sprawled across the entrance, Sela stirred. Obsessed with his craving, Xie had not noticed the electric current that shot through his prisoner's body, when he mentioned the 'Garhwalis…'

No sooner had the officer left than Sela jumped off the cot and started to follow him out of the tent. But she had barely taken two steps into the sunshine when a sentry barred her way, 'Where are you going, beautiful girl? The Senior Captain did not say anything about you leaving this tent, eh?'

She tried to push past the man. But he slung his rifle over his back, and called out to his companion. Together, the soldiers grabbed both her hands and pulled her gently but firmly back into her prison.

'Now you sit down here…and be a good girl. You don't want to get shot like that old woman, do you?'

Sela went back into her shell. She refused to eat any food that day, despite the sentries' threats. By and by, dusk threw his wintry sheet over the military camp. Sela was lying upon the cot on her side, face turned away from the tent's flaps. She could hear the guards walking up and down outside the tent, and their whispered conversation.

Then, she sensed, rather than heard the shuffle of soft footsteps approaching her. But she did not turn to see, knowing it would be some slave bringing her another meal, trying to make her eat so the officer would find his prisoner in good health when he returned to try and break through her defences.

Gentle fingers touched her shoulder, said, 'Eat, girl. Are you a prisoner… too…?'

When she heard that voice, Sela's body went rigid for a moment. Then she twisted slowly around upon the bed, and looked at the woman who had brought her food.

Was she hallucinating?

'Sister!' exclaimed the other woman, and Sela knew this

was no dream. Noora, her doting sister, leaned over the captive with a plate of food in her hands.

'Noora!' she said hoarsely, then putting a finger on her lips, 'Shh! Shh!' she pointed toward the tent's exit. Sitting up, Sela threw her arms about her sister's shoulders and hugged her.

'Wait...wait...' Noora extricated herself from that desperate embrace and took a step back. Breast heaving, she gazed incredulously at her younger sibling. Then she nodded, and placing the plate of food upon the bed, she started to take off her cap, belt, the blue gown and her chemise.

'What... are you doing... sister?' Sela jumped to her feet.

'Quick! Do as I say. Quick...wear these clothes...now!'

Mutely, without quite comprehending what Noora meant to do, Sela obeyed her sister's instructions. When she had also undressed, Noora snatched up her sister's clothes and started to put them on.

'But...sister...I don't...what are you doing?'

'Quiet!' Noora looked at Sela and jerked her head. 'Wear these clothes. Now! Don't ask questions, little one. Just do as I say.'

Sela obeyed. When they had exchanged their clothes, Noora made Sela sit down and they quickly wolfed down the meal from the platter. She knew the importance of eating when setting out on a journey.

Then, Noora pulled her sister close, clasping her to her bosom once more. 'Now go, little one. Take that plate and go outside. Do not look at the guards. Just keep your head bowed and they will not see anything amiss. Leave... quickly!'

Sela would have protested, but Noora had already taken her place on the cot, with her face turned away. Sela bent and kissed her sister upon the head. Then, muttering a prayer, she picked up the empty plate and left the tent.

❦

The first wave of Chinese came at 0400 hrs. They opened up with mortar and small arms fire. Before long, their heavy artillery began to probe the Indian positions.

'*Hoshiyar!*' shouted the Subedar, 'Positions, men! Man your positions. Hold your fire until I give the word.'

Sure enough, the round blue fur caps of the PLA could be seen bobbing in the distance, trying to get as close to the Indian lines as they might be able to while their cannon kept the Indians under pressure.

Soon, the Chinese came within range of the Indian guns and a fusillade caught them.

'*Jai Badri Vishaal*! Give them hell!' bellowed Udai Singh.

'*Jai Badri Vishaal*!' the Garhwalis took up the battle cry, and sent another withering volley at the attackers. The Indians' fire was too accurate for the Chinese to withstand for any length of time. They withdrew, but many Chinese would not fight again.

'Everyone all right?'

Only a couple of his men had minor bullet wounds, the Subedar noted with relief. The platoon settled down to wait. The Chinese would return. They did, four hours later at 0800 hrs. Their numbers were greater, this time. Once again, Udai Singh's men raked the rocks ahead of them with accurate fire, and the attack buckled, then broke. The number of the Chinese dead was even greater in this assault. But some of the Garhwalis had fired their last bullets, too.

'They will be back, Sir,' the Subedar spoke to his Company Commander over the radio. The morning was already bright blue, and the Chinese preparations were clearly visible. 'There are a great many of them…more than regiment strength. I do not know how long my men will be able to hold them off, but we shall sell our lives dearly, Saabji. *Jai Badri Vishaal*!'

'Good man,' replied 2nd Lt Tandon. 'I'm in touch with Brigade. Maybe they will send us some relief. Those Sikhs are not far away. If they join us…but, we can't depend on that happening, Subedar. May the Lord be with you and your men, Udai Singh. *Jai Badri Vishaal*!'

Sela left her sister with trepidation. But her self-doubt, and the slow steps that took her away from the tent where her sister was now imprisoned, only lulled the guards' suspicions, if they had any.

One of the guards even said, 'If you're not too busy tonight, girl…you come to us. When the Senior Captain is busy with his mistress…what…what?'

The guards' guffaws followed Sela as she left them behind. It took a great effort for her not to take to her heels, as long as she was within their sights. But once she thought she was safely away, the girl began to hurry, taking care always not to attract attention. It helped that there was a drizzle, and the Chinese soldiers and their Tibetan and Monpa slaves had taken cover. She had no fear of any Monpa recognizing her and sounding an alarm, for they would only think that she too was a slave, and employed by the Chinese invaders.

But as she reached the edge of the Chinese encampment, and approached the Bridge on the Tawang Chu, Sela realized that she would have to be careful. The riverfront on both banks was crawling with soldiers.

She disappeared behind some rhododendron bushes for a while. Anyone who noticed her do so would presume she was getting out of sight to relieve herself.

Once out of reach of prying eyes, though, Sela began to climb. Her keen, young eyes had already noticed a mithun track leading up towards a cliff that overlooked the bridge. The drizzle and dark made climbing slow and difficult work, and soon her chemise was torn and her knees and elbows were bruised due to constant abrasion against rock.

But she had no time to waste on these minor inconveniences. The Chinese army was waiting, perhaps for orders. Once the fighting resumed, there would be little chance of her being able to cross that bridge or the road that lay beyond the Jang-Se La route. And somewhere on that path, god only knew how near or how far away, were the Indians, and among them her man.

She would have to make her move *now*. There was a group of soldiers just beyond the bridge. From what she could make out at this distance, those men were relaxing and chatting. On the near side of the bridge, not far from where she watched them, was a group of Tibetan and Monpa slaves, who appeared to be busy preparing food and packing it. As Sela watched, one woman loaded packages of food and cans of water upon a yak. When the yak's saddlebags were piled high, this slave took the animal's rope and moved toward the soldiers at the foot of the bridge.

That gave Sela an idea. Five minutes later, she had scrambled down from her high perch and was mixing with the slaves, as if she were one among them. With her grime stained features and tattered clothing, no one suspected that this young girl was an intruder.

Taking a deep breath, she made up her mind, and grabbed

the lead rope of a waiting yak. A minute later, she was mingling with the group of servants who were cooking and packing the food.

'You, there!' she started at the shouted command from a cook, but then gathered her wits and moved forward with her pack animal. 'Here… load up this food and water. It's all for those men across the bridge, you understand?'

Sela nodded and began loading the compact packages upon the yak.

'Go, quickly. Before those soldiers lose their temper over the delay in feeding them and come over here to vent their anger on us. Move, woman…'

Sela did not need any more urging. Taking the yak's halter rope, she began to move towards the bridge on the Tawang Chu. Ten minutes more and she had crossed over, and was among the soldiers who constituted the picket on the Southern bank of the river. The soldiers laughed and joked while she distributed the food and water, some of them even trying to grab her arms or slapping her buttocks in their boisterousness. She did not react, knowing that she was expected to behave like a slave. If these men suspected a trick, they would as easily shoot or bayonet her.

When she had finished handing out the food packets there were still a few left on the yak's saddlebags, and so she started to move off, in the direction of the Se La road.

'Hey, where are you going?' called a soldier and started forward, as if to bring her back. For an instant, Sela froze, and her fingers went rigid on the lead rope. 'There's no one there to feed. Come back…'

'Leave her alone!' said a second voice. This belonged to someone in authority, obviously a superior. His words stopped the soldier who had made a move towards the slave woman. 'She's probably taken those extra packets for herself, poor thing…wants to sit somewhere out of sight and fill her stomach. Can't you see how dead beat the woman looks? Let her be…'

Sela had deliberately loaded a couple of extra food packages on the yak so that she could leave the soldiers guarding the bridge after she gave them their meals on the pretext that she was going to feed others, further down the road. She had not imagined that there might be no more Chinese soldiers there.

'Or maybe she's going to find some of those Indians to feed…poor suckers. Maybe some of them got left behind when their comrades ran for their lives… eh… heh… ha ha ha…'

There was a burst of harsh laughter from the soldiers. Taking advantage of their distraction, Sela moved slowly, deliberately away with the yak. She had seen a heavy clump of vegetation. The soldiers were no longer paying her any attention. Still, she had to behave as if she were only seeking a quiet place to sit down and eat her meal, as the Sergeant had presumed.

Once she was out of sight of the soldiers, Sela abandoned the yak. Her eyes examined the mountainside and the scrub forest around. Presently, her mountain and jungle-trained eyes located another mithun trail, leading through a declivity. The sounds of conversation and laughter, and the other noises coming from the Chinese camp across the river, began to subside until she could eventually hear nothing, except the chirping of insects in the thickets or the shuffling of her own feet.

Although she was tired and would have liked to sit down for a while and partake of the food inside the package, she had retrieved from the yak's saddlebags, Sela realized that she must waste no time. She trudged through the night, until after some time she found herself crossing an open ground. She had barely traversed the exposed stretch when she heard loud explosions. Terrified, she dived for cover. But then, she realized that no one was trying to kill her. Yet, the gunfire was close by. That meant the Chinese and Indians were fighting. If so, were the Indian soldiers Garhwalis? Was her Jaswant among the defenders?

Carefully, she raised her head skyward. The silken blue black over the jagged mountains told her it was almost dawn.

# 18

When Thabo arrived at the Chinese camp, he was relieved. But there was no cause to celebrate yet. First, he had to locate at least one of the girls. In the course of his journey up to this point, the yak herder had come to a decision. If he was eventually unable to find Noora and bring her before the Chinese officer, he would, instead, try to free Sela from the clutches of her captors. There could be no other way. In doing so, he would be staking his life. But on the other hand, he saw no point in living if he could not even find and secure one of the sisters as his life's companion. He was in love with Sela, but Noora would do as well. As a matter of fact, she would make the ideal wife. Every conscientious yak herder needed a good, reliable woman to tend to his house and children when he was away in the hills looking after his herd, often for weeks at a stretch.

Thabo noticed several familiar faces among the camp followers of the Chinese. During their stay in Tawang town, the invaders had drafted into their entourage many of the Monpa population. He now moved among these people, discreetly enquiring about Noora and Sela's whereabouts. He spent a few hours wandering about and questioning the Monpas, but without success. By and by, tired after his exhausting journey and dispirited by the lack of a breakthrough, the herder was on the point of giving up, when his eyes fell upon a figure walking towards one of the better-quality tents in the camp. It was a woman, carrying a tray. A…woman… but that wasn't just any Tibetan or Monpa woman. Yes, it was…Noora! He would recognize her gait anywhere. He was on the point of calling out to her, but just in time he bit back the words that were about to explode from his lips.

What was Noora doing here? Why was she entering that tent? Now that he had located her, he decided to be patient, and investigate further. He had not long to wait, for some time later, she emerged from the tent carrying the presumably empty plate. But there was still no immediate possibility of his accosting her, for two armed sentries had appeared near the tent.

Gnashing his teeth in frustration and wringing his hands, Thabo watched Noora moving away from the tent. Then his heart did a double take. His palms went suddenly dry.

By all the gods…that was not Noora! In fact… that could only be… but…his eyes strained, trying to see the woman's features through the thin rain and twilight. As his eyes got accustomed to the weakening light and the woman's physiognomy, his jaw dropped. Sela! But how…yet, that had to be Sela. Anyone else might be taken in, given the striking similarity between the girls, but not Thabo. He had seen them grow up, watched their bodies become strong and nubile. How he had hungered for an affectionate smile and touch from this Sela!

So here she was, at last. But what were the girls up to? Noora had entered the tent, while the one that came out was Sela. Even the yak herder's unhurried mental processes could figure out the deception. They had switched clothes! And Sela was escaping, without a doubt.

Now the soldiers were talking aloud to Sela, their gazes following her, although she appeared to ignore their calls. One of the sentries, in fact, wandered off some distance behind the girl. This was no time to interfere, decided Thabo. Not yet.

But he was now caught in a cleft stick. Should he pursue Sela, and take her back with him, or wait here and find out more about the sisters' ruse? But he had a hunch where Sela would go, once she left this place. He could always follow her in that direction when he wished and catch up. Thabo had not the slightest doubt that the Indians were far away by now. The Chinese army would reach them before Sela did, and not one of those Indian soldiers was going to be alive in any case, when this war ended.

The herder cursed under his breath, trying to drag his attention back to the tent. He would wait for as long as it took him to discover Noora's scheme. Retreating behind a pile of supplies, where no wandering soldier might find him, Thabo waited.

He was getting impatient, and was on the verge of moving out of his cover, when the smart figure of an officer marched up to the tent. The sentries snapped to attention, saluting this officer. Thabo recognized Senior Captain Xie and was more confused than ever. Here was he, having spent over twenty-four hours trying to track down Noora so that he might hand her over to the Chinese officer in exchange for Sela. And to think that the girl had, quite willingly it seemed, walked into the officer's arms!

Presently, the light inside the tent became brighter, but only a few minutes later he heard the Senior Captain's voice raised in anger, and the sentries scrambled into the tent. Then, they rushed out again and disappeared into the surrounding gloom, and it was obvious that the trick had been discovered and they were going to look for the escaped woman.

Still Thabo waited, and his patience was rewarded when a soldier ran up to the tent and called. Xie emerged, looking angry. After a hurried conversation with the messenger, the officer also stalked away from the tent. It appeared that there was some military emergency.

Thabo took a few deep breaths, looking around. Then, he left his hiding place and started forward. He was glad for the steady drizzle, and reached the tent safely. Noora was slumped on the floor of the tent, head bowed. Her hands had been tied to a tent pole.

'Noora!' he called softly, 'Noora…it's me!'

She looked up, and for a moment she seemed dazed. Then recognition dawned, and a tremulous smile appeared on her lips.

'Quick, Noora! Quickly…' he sat down by her and with his machete he slashed her bonds. 'We have to leave this place. Hurry!'

Like wraiths, they glided out of the tent and soon merged with the hills that were their home. When they were far enough from the camp, Noora suddenly stopped.

'What…' the herder looked at her in surprise. 'What's the matter? We must keep moving if we are to get home before they find us.'

She shook her head. 'No, you go home. I must go and find them.'

'Who…what are you talking about? Have you taken leave of your senses? If the Chinese catch you again…'

'They will not,' she said with a quiet determination, and

he realized there was no point trying to dissuade her.

For a moment, a great, towering rage possessed the herder, a man normally slow to anger. She appeared to sense the rush of emotion within him, and she grasped both his hands, firmly, reassuringly. 'I have to do this...and you must help me.'

He shook his head, as if trying to clear his wits, get a hold on himself.

'Please go back and get some food. I am going on...you follow, with the food and water.' She took a deep, shuddering breath, 'Afterwards...I will be your woman...forever.'

'But...where are you going, girl?'

Her eyes shone like glow-worms in the night, and he understood.

'Take my mule,' he said, turning away from her, 'I...I can walk.'

'Look!' shouted one of the sentries on the right flank of the feature where Udai Singh's Garhwali platoon were entrenched. He was pointing towards the slope facing them. 'There's something moving out there.'

'Could be a wild animal,' said his partner.

'A wild beast close to eleven in the morning...in broad daylight? Could be the Chinese...?'

'Maybe...but the Chinese don't send out scouts like this. What...'

The soldiers' curiosity was resolved a moment later when a human figure appeared through the scrub, scrambling down the slope into a gully, then up the rocky path to where Udai Singh's platoon was perched in their trenches and bunkers.

'Hey, that looks like...it is...a woman!'

'Look at that uniform. It's a Tibetan slave...'

'Or a Monpa...who knows...they all look alike to me.'

'But what's she doing here?' said one of the sentries as he lined his rifle upon the approaching figure.

'Wait...don't fire!' said his mate, 'Let's take her to the Subedar first.'

Udai Singh stared grimly at the woman facing him. She was clad in the loose, blue uniform worn by the Tibetan slaves that the Chinese employed. Her dress was torn at places, and her hair beneath the wide cap dishevelled.

'What are you doing here?' asked the Subedar. 'In wartime, spies are shot...'

The woman's eyes gleamed, and she replied, 'Sela... Jaswant...'

'What...did you say?' for a moment the JCO was caught off guard by the seemingly irrelevant reply.

'She said Jaswant, Saabji!' exclaimed one of the sentries, round-eyed with astonishment.

'Jaswant? What on earth...who are you?'

'Sela,' she touched her chest with her forefinger then pointed, 'Jaswant...'

'Saabji...I...I think this is...Jaswant's girl! That...that Monpa...'

Sela nodded vigorously, as if she understood what they were discussing.

'Should we tell...Jaswant about this, Saabji?' asked one of the sentries in excitement.

'No, wait. Not now. He's in that bunker out front. The Chinese are going to attack. I don't want my men distracted. Watch her...and don't let her out of your sight until this is finished...' and the Subedar hurried off.

As if to fulfil the JCO's prophesy, the Chinese batteries unleashed a barrage a couple of minutes later.

But on this their third assault, the attackers seemed to have learned their lesson. The heavy artillery bombardment was relentless this time, pinning the Indians down. Taking advantage, the Chinese brought up a Medium Machine Gun. Precisely at 1100 hrs, the MMG began to chatter, casting a blanket of deadly fire upon the Indians. Udai Singh's platoon was trapped, unable to counter-attack or even to raise their heads as long as the machine gun was trained upon their positions.

Udai Singh was in one of the forward bunkers, directing the defence. He turned to the wireless operator standing behind, 'Is there any news from Company Commander?'

When the jawan shook his head, the Subedar shrugged. He glanced quickly about, at the anxious faces of his soldiers. He had already lost some men to the MMG. He couldn't afford to lose more.

'We have to silence that gun, men…before it is too late.'

Lance Naik Trilok Singh Negi spoke up, 'I'll go, Saabji… alone…'

'Says who?' Gopal Gusain grimaced through the gun smoke. 'You may have written your last will and testament, Negi, but remember that I cannot die. I am immortal, as our mate here says…' he winked at Jaswant.

Jaswant gazed at his friends. He also knew that attacking the MMG was inviting death. For a moment, he was torn between loyalty to his comrades and the desire to stay alive so that he could see his Sela, one last time.

'*Jai Badri Vishaal*!' he exclaimed, and jumped to his feet. 'Here, give me a few more of those grenades. These rifles will only slow us down. We have to crawl up that slope.'

'You don't have to go, Jaswant,' said the JCO. 'I don't have too many men to spare.'

Jaswant flipped open the pocket of his woollen shirt. Taking out the neatly folded inland letter, he now handed it over to the Subedar, 'Company Commander wanted me to give this to you, Saabji.'

Udai Singh gazed at Rifleman Jaswant Singh Rawat with a strange look in his eyes, as if he were on the point of saying something. Then he turned and snapped, 'Take the LMG, Negi! We'll give you covering fire...go when I give the word.'

Suddenly, the Indians let fly upwards from their bunkers, giving it everything they had. At the same moment, the three volunteers burst from cover, scrambling down the slope. Soon, they were sprinting towards the rock face where the Chinese MMG was located, dodging behind stone and scrub and using every inch of available cover.

At ten yards from the enemy position, Trilok Singh stopped and set up his LMG. His trigger finger squeezed, and bullets thudded into the Chinese bunker. Jaswant and Gopal crawled forward. Suddenly, Gopal reared to his feet and threw his grenades, one after the other, at the gun position. But a burst from the MMG caught him, and the grenades exploded harmlessly outside the bunker.

'Gopal!' exclaimed Jaswant, panic-stricken and momentarily undecided whether to go to his fallen comrade or press on with his mission.

Then another volley from the MMG found Trilok Singh Negi. Jaswant saw his NCO's body bucking under the impact of the bullets. No man could survive those many bullets.

Jaswant was on his own now. The MMG continued to chatter, pounding the bunkers where his colleagues were crouched, unable to raise their heads under its lethal fire.

'Come back, Jas…want!' he heard the Subedar's voice, almost drowned in the gunfire, 'You can still make it back… hurry!'

Suddenly, Sela's kind, pretty face rose before his mind's eye, and Jaswant jumped to his feet with a bellow of *'Jai Badri Vishaal! Bharat Mata ki Jai*!' He was facing the MMG position now, directly in its line of fire. Miraculously, its bullets appeared to fly past him. Almost in a dream, his teeth ripped the pins out of the grenades, one by one, and his arms swept in arcs as the egg-shaped messengers of death flew unerringly towards their target.

Then a terrible blow slammed into his head and he fell. Even as his body crumpled, Jaswant heard two muffled 'bangs', then a third, earth-shattering explosion. He did not see the MMG being catapulted out of the bunker, followed by the dismembered bodies of the men inside.

# 19

Subedar Udai Singh Rawat could not believe his ears. In less than twenty-four hours, his platoon had withstood four attacks from the Chinese. One full battalion of the enemy, armed with semi-automatics and machine guns and backed up by mortar and heavy artillery, had been trying to pound the handful of Garhwalis into submission. Still they held out, licking their wounds and mourning their dead, proud of the trio who had charged and destroyed the MMG during the third Chinese attack.

Udai Singh's frantic calls to Company Commander for ammunition were answered; one brave officer risked his life and arrived with the ordnance. Too little, and maybe too late. Still, thought the Subedar, something to give the platoon hope.

The Chinese had not dared return to attack 'A' Company after the beating they received at the hands of Udai Singh's men. However, they were not about to give up. The Subedar knew that the battalion thrown at him was only a foretaste of things to come. With Bridge 4 back in working order, the invaders were now repairing the road damaged in the shelling. This only indicated that they would soon bring forward more of their heavy weapons. And the rest of the Chinese regiment was going to cross the bridge, sooner rather than later.

During their last conversation, Udai Singh had reiterated his request to his commander to ask for the Sikhs on the left bank to be sent forward to his aid. If that happened, if one full company of Indians could take up positions here, there was no saying what they might not achieve. That would also give the Brigade at Se La time enough to prepare a detailed defensive plan. This, after all, might be just the break the Indian forces had been looking for, these past couple of months. Was this going to be the mother of all battles, a day the Chinese would live to rue?

Minutes stretched into hours. The Lieutenant who brought him the ammunition was long gone. For a while, the Company Commander kept telling Udai Singh to wait, that he was still talking to Brigade about the possibility of sending a company to relieve, or at least to bolster, their strength. But after a while the commander stopped answering the radio altogether.

The Subedar walked among his men, trying to cheer them up, enquiring about their wounds and health.

At 1700 hrs, the radio crackled again. 2nd Lt Tandon's sombre tones said, 'Udai Singh, you will withdraw immediately to Se La Pass. See that there is no panic. Carry your weapons and ammunition and whatever supplies you can take.'

'B...but... Saabji... we... we...'

'1 Sikhs and later 4 Sikh LI will cover your retreat. We are leaving now. We'll see you all at Se La, Udai Singh. God be with you...and your brave men. *Jai Badri Vishaal*!'

As the Company Commander's voice died out over the airwaves, followed by a prolonged burst of static, there was stunned silence in the bunker. Udai Singh and his men gazed at one another, no one quite knowing how to break the tension.

Gopal Singh Gusain, barely conscious, groaned, 'Where…is Jaswant? Negi…Trilok Singh Negi…where are you…'

Gopal lay on a stretcher in one corner of the dimly-lit bunker, his head, chest and legs swathed in bandages. One eye was obscured by a bloodied bandage, and the other gleamed dully in the gloom inside the bunker.

No one answered. Not one man in that small group had the heart to tell Gopal that he had been to hell and back. The miracle was that he lived, to tell the tale. As for his good friends—Trilok Singh Negi and Jaswant Singh Rawat—the curtain had fallen on their lives in this world, and their families would now hear of them only when the stories of their valour rang out in the hills of their native Garhwal.

As the Subedar walked away from the bunker, one of the sentries approached and saluted. 'The woman…Saabji. Jaswant's…er…the Monpa…what do we do with her?'

Udai Singh looked fixedly at his subordinate for a long minute, then shook his head. 'Nothing. Just…let her go.'

❦

By the time Noora reached the riverbank, guns had started to boom. Fortunately, most of the Chinese had moved across the bridge. She was able to cross without too much difficulty.

She couldn't wait for the fighting to end, so she pressed on, avoiding the road and the people. Climbing the slopes across the Tawang Chu, she trudged on, as night merged into a pale dawn, then became the white, remorseless light of another cold, violent day.

The lull in the sounds of gunfire was no cause for celebration, she realized. And she was right; more of it followed. 'Who was winning?' she wondered. Did it matter?

There was no way she was going to be able to investigate the fate of a battle that mattered little to her. But as soon as the thought crossed her mind, she knew it wasn't entirely true. There was one person there, probably, whose well-being mattered to her. Two, if her sister had actually managed to reach the Garhwali lines.

It was almost evening when she reached a vantage point from where she could actually see the flashes of the cannon, and hear the deep boom of the heavy guns interspersed with the rattle of machine guns. She could discern figures moving between bunkers, scurrying back and forth, sometimes hiding, sometimes exposed.

A strange rumbling surprised her. Then she realized it was her stomach. She hadn't eaten, since that last, hasty meal shared with her sister. But food would have to wait until she could get close to the Indian lines, if at all that were possible, or something else came her way.

As sunlight faded and the evening settled in, she began to feel weak with hunger. Deciding it was now or never, she started the descent towards the scene of the recent battle. After a while, she lost sight of her objective, but she knew the general direction she had to take. The sun had almost set, when she stumbled upon a couple of bodies lying on a grassy slope. They were Chinese, she judged from the uniforms. She retreated quickly into the cover of a rhododendron thicket, to make sure the dead soldiers' comrades weren't about. But after a while of waiting she realized nothing stirred, in the still evening. Even the breeze of the daytime had subsided.

Emerging from her cover, then, she quickly looked in the dead soldiers' pouches, and was relieved to find some food. She also found a canteen with a little water left in it. She ate ravenously, and drank all the water.

As she stood up, preparing to resume her journey into the unknown, she became aware that it was now dark. The question that possessed her was, where were the Indians? She was now certain the Garhwalis had made a stand here. But, where were they now? Had they been overwhelmed and slaughtered? But she hadn't found any Indian dead so far. Dared she hope...maybe Jaswant and his colleagues had fallen back to Se La?

She was still wrestling with this question, when she heard a sound. Barely audible, she probably only noticed it because it was not of a piece with the other noises of night. Her keen ears caught it again...a growl. Immediately, she dropped to her knees and began to move slowly in the direction from where she thought the sound had come. There was another slope, after a dip, barely ten metres away. She had not noticed it because of the heavy vegetation there.

A moment later, she was picking her way through bramble, trying to move noiselessly in the dark. Was that a wild animal? She did not know why she was taking such a chance, or wasting time here, when she ought to have been pushing on, following the retreating Indians, if they had indeed retreated. She had to get to the Garhwalis before it was too late. An instinct told her she would find Sela there. Where else could her sister go?

She did not even pause to consider the possibility that the war had claimed their lives. That just could not happen. There was something she had to do.

Suddenly, she heard a low growl. It rolled like the gurgle of a stream, but in a terrifying sort of way. Gently, noiselessly, she pulled apart the intertwined bushes that obscured her view. Beyond, she sensed, was the source of that sound.

When the thickets parted, her eyes took in the scene before

her, and the beating of her heart slowed. Fingers trembled, and in the darkness, her lips blanched. Her keen, young eyes had spotted the predator. A snow leopard. The beast was stalking its prey, something out there, in the open.

She sensed she was upwind of the predator and for the moment safe from discovery. But retreat she would not, even to save her life. Some instinct goaded her on, to investigate what it was the cat hunted.

Her eyes were tiring now, eyelids heavy with lack of sleep. Yet her gaze probed the night. Then the moon burst forth from a cloud veil, and light splashed upon the clearing. She would probably have recognized the prone figure, even if it were pitch dark.

After all, it had been night when they last met, and were torn apart by the truth that their love had been a lie.

# 20

As soon as the Indian sentries cut Sela's bonds and told her by their words and gestures that she was free, she rushed out of the bunker where she had been kept. For a while, she ran back and forth between the scattered bunkers and the trenches.

No one appeared to pay any attention to her. Or maybe, it was by design that the Garhwalis ignored her, now. But if she had been hoping to catch a glimpse of Jaswant's friends Gopal and Trilok, that was not to be, either.

Heart palpitating, exhausted by all her recent travel and the emotional overload of being so near and yet so far from her Jaswant, she stood panting in the fading light of evening, watching the Garhwalis. The soldiers appeared to be strangely dispirited, their shoulders sagging, no more exchanging the friendly smiles and banter she had become accustomed to, whenever she met any of the soldiers.

Then, the truth dawned upon her. They were leaving. The Garhwalis were abandoning their trenches and bunkers. But where was Jaswant? Was he also going away?

In her desperation, she sought the Subedar, and found him at last, supervising the arrangements for an orderly retreat. Rushing at the JCO, she grabbed him by his woollen shirt and shook him, saying, 'Jaswant…Jaswant…where is Jaswant?'

At this, a couple of soldiers rushed forward with raised weapons, but Udai Singh shook his head, as if telling his colleagues to let her be.

The veteran of many battles looked briefly into those young, frantic eyes. He disengaged himself from her grip, gently yet firmly. Then, he took a piece of folded paper from his shirt pocket and placed it in the young woman's fist, before turning and walking away.

Sela stood for a long, gut-wrenching minute watching the Subedar's retreating back, and now she understood the meaning of his silence. For a moment, she looked at the folded blue inland letter in her palm, then with a scream she turned and rushed away from the Garhwalis, calling Jaswant's name, the blue Tibetan coat flapping behind her.

Scrambling down slopes and up rock faces, she searched for her lost beloved. It was Trilok Singh Negi whom she stumbled across first. Although it was dusk, she recognized Jaswant's friend's features as soon as she laid eyes on the bullet riddled body. The martyr lay still, impervious to the sounds of his retreating platoon, or even the banshee wind that picked up force as the night waned.

She laid her ears to the fallen soldier's breast. But he breathed no more. Yet, hope revived in her breast, that maybe she was going to find Jaswant also. What if he was lying wounded, and close by?

She got up and again rushed wildly back and forth, frantic with hope and terror. But it was dark now, and she could see no more the traces of the battle that had ripped apart this mountain so recently.

Exhausted and dispirited, she returned once more to sit by Trilok's lifeless figure, as if by some miracle it would come alive and tell her the whereabouts of her Jaswant.

That was the moment when she heard the scream.

There is something about siblings; they can smell, sense one another even in the most distracting circumstances. Long before the echoes of that single scream had died out, Sela was sprinting in the direction from which it originated.

As she came thrusting to her feet, almost without thinking her right hand fumbled in the night and found a jagged piece of stone. With an answering yell of anger mixed with fear, she launched herself through the rhododendron bushes that screened the origin of the first scream.

She glimpsed Noora's kneeling figure, in the same instant that the predator pounced. Without a second thought, Sela launched the sharp rock, and followed it up with her body. The boldness of that unprecedented onslaught was too much for the beast. The heavy rock hit the animal's pelt before Sela's weight knocked the wind out of it. Snarling and clawing, the leopard twisted like a dancer. Then, as Noora also came out of her paralysis and leaped into the fray, the leopard let out a frustrated snarl and bounded into the rocks, leaving behind the meal that was not to be.

A moment later, the sisters were hugging and kissing one another in relief at the threat neutralized. By and by, their emotion subsided, and Sela's eyes wandered to the object that Noora had been examining, when the wild animal attacked her.

Sela needed no second look to recognize the figure stretched on the ground.

'Jaswant!' she screamed, 'Jaswant...' and she lifted his head and cradled it in her lap, sobs of anguish racking her body.

Noora placed a comforting hand upon her sister's shoulder, 'Shh! Not so loud, little one…there may be Chinese soldiers about. Be quiet…'

Bleary-eyed in defeat, Sela gazed at her sister. 'I found him,' her expression seemed to say, but too late.

Noora's eyes read the look, and she shook her head, 'No, little one. He lives. Yes…he breathes.'

It was true. Despite the coldness of his skin and the pallor of his face, Sela discovered, Jaswant still had a faint pulse. His breath flowed still, although it was weak, and he was unconscious. Lovingly, she caressed the wound where the bullet from the machine gun had grazed his temple. She dared not remove the caked blood, though, for fear she might set off the bleeding again.

Meanwhile, leaving Sela to fuss over the insensible figure of the soldier, the older sister marched off into the dark to survey the neighbourhood, and their present circumstances.

She fetched Thabo's mule from where she had left him tied beyond the thickets. The sisters were so exhausted with all the exertion of the past couple of days that it took a combined, superhuman effort, and the provocation of intense love, for them to lift the jawan's deadweight on to the animal's back.

Then, taking the mule's halter rope, Noora led the way towards the intimidating outlines of a high outcrop that she had discerned, in the moonlight. There they would have a view of the road below, she had decided, and no one would be able to approach without warning.

As for Sela, she followed her sister mutely. She now had eyes only for her lover's body draped across the mule's back.

The cliff top had probably been a defensive position occupied by the Indians, before they left. There were bunkers gouged into the rock and earth of the mountain all around. Running parallel to the edge of the cliff was a long trench.

Together, the sisters carried Jaswant into one of the bunkers. Finding a little bit of kerosene in a battered can and a discarded box of matches, Noora lit a lantern. Its chimney was shattered, but the lamp worked. Fortunately, although the night was awfully cold, there was no breeze.

By the unwavering flame of the kerosene lamp, Sela sat down upon the cold floor of the bunker, with her back against a crude wall and Jaswant's unmoving head in her lap.

Noora, meanwhile, took the mule and picked her way carefully down the almost concealed track that had helped them climb to this elevated feature. A few minutes later, she was back at the spot where she had found Jaswant.

She did not quite know what she was looking for. But soon she found the MMG lying entangled in bushes where the impact of the explosion had thrown it. She almost shouted for joy. Now she had a weapon, although if it came to a fight for survival she had no idea how the two of them were going to use it, without Jaswant's help. She did understand, though, that she would need cartridges for the machine gun. Casting a glance around, she noticed the remains of the smashed bunker inside which the Chinese had positioned the MMG, during that fatal skirmish. She tethered the mule and clambered quickly up the slope and into this cavity, where she saw two heavy boxes. She guessed that they contained shells. She also saw a couple of rifles, amid the ruins. As she was turning away, she noticed a bottle thrown in a corner. Examining it, she found it was rum, and the bottle was still half-full. She slipped this into a pocket of her chemise.

With much huffing and puffing, she dragged the ammunition

boxes down the slope to the mule. One by one, she lifted and tied the machine gun and the wooden boxes securely upon the animal's back, using the sash on her chemise to fasten them. The rifles she carried, one slung upon each shoulder.

Just as she bent to pick up the mule's reins, a heavy hand fell upon her shoulder. She gasped, and might have screamed, had a powerful palm not been clapped over her mouth.

'Shh! It is me, Thabo!'

With a deep, shuddering sigh of relief, she pushed him away. He did not resist.

The yak herder at this moment was an angel come to the rescue.

'What are you doing here?' he asked with a suspicious glint in his eyes, pointing to the mule, 'And what is all this you are carrying?'

'Did you…' she panted, 'Did you get the food and water?'

He nodded, 'Of course I did. What do you take me for…I know these hills better than anyone else.'

He held out a heavy satchel, and a couple of water canisters, 'Here's food…and water. But…what do you want with it? Have you…should we not return home now? I know…I know that the Indians were defeated and they have run away. Most of them were killed, I think.'

Her eyes darted to the top of the knoll, and he followed her gaze. Then, he understood. 'Who…who is it…up there?'

In response, she took from him the satchel containing food and hung it on the mule's back. The water canisters she slung across one shoulder, saying, 'I…I found them…'

A mixture of hope and frustration flashed in his eyes. He rumbled, 'Is…he…'

She took a step forward and clutched his hands. Squeezing

his rough, calloused palms, she breathed, 'I…there is one thing more you must do for me.'

He looked incredulously at her, as if unable to comprehend her persistence in this mad venture. 'No more…I can do no more…'

'I am now your wife, and I ask you to do this for me.'

He stood quiet, looking her up and down, then shook his head like an inarticulate, disconsolate beast of burden.

'Go to the monastery and bring the Khempo. Tell him it is *my* request. He will understand, and he will follow you. I know.'

'But…this is crazy!' he exclaimed, 'Why should the Khempo…besides, I cannot leave you alone here anymore. The Chinese…the Chinese are still in the vicinity.'

'You know I will be safe. I know these mountains almost as well as you do. Go quickly, and hurry back.'

# 21

When Noora returned to the hilltop, she found that Sela was asleep, with Jaswant's head still in her lap. So, she went off again into the thickets dotting the hillside and gathered leaves and twigs. When she thought she had enough material, she returned with these to the bunker and made a couple of pillows, side by side.

Gently lifting Jaswant's head from her sister's lap, she laid him upon one of these makeshift mattresses, before doing likewise with Sela. Noora was grateful her sibling was so exhausted that she did not wake up, with all the pulling and pushing.

Afterwards, she sat down by Jaswant's side, and tearing pieces of cloth from her underskirt, she soaked them in a little water from the containers Thabo had brought, and cleaned Jaswant's wound tenderly, taking care not to wake him in the course of her ministrations. Then, she unbuttoned his shirt and sponged his torso as well as she could.

She wondered at how weak and drawn he appeared, not at all like the sturdy soldier who would present himself before her whenever she visited the military camp. If only she had with her some of the churpi he loved so much.

When she had finished attending to her unconscious patient, the young woman sat down with her back against a cold, hard wall inside the bunker and shut her eyes. She needed to catch her breath, until it became time again to attend to him and her little sister.

But the moment her eyes closed, Noora slept.

Sela was the first to wake up, stirred by the sound of birds. When her eyes snapped open at this pastoral medley, she was alarmed. Daylight played outside the bunker. Her eyes widened in terror as she recalled events of the night before, wildly seeking Jaswant when she realized his head was not on her lap.

But then she saw him resting peacefully, his head on the leafy pillow, snoring softly, and she almost laughed in relief. Her sister was still asleep, leaning against one of the walls of the bunker.

Getting quickly to her feet, Sela found the water canisters, and splashed a little bit of the water on her face. Then, she gathered more wood and twigs and lit a fire with the matches Noora had saved the night before. She found meat in the satchel and boiled it in one of the canisters to make soup. Taking Jaswant's head once more into her lap, she inserted the soup between his lips. Even in sleep his throat worked, as the warm liquid slid down his gullet. Her heart ached at the thought of all the hours that he had lain there, wounded and helpless, without food or water.

But now she was with him, and she would care for him, even take him back home. Gently, she rocked him in her lap, and in doing so, she fell asleep again.

'Where...am I? Where am I? Mother...mother...is that you?'

It was Noora who woke up first to hear the convalescent's mumbling. As soon as her eyes opened she realized it was

Jaswant speaking. Then she saw his head in Sela's lap. They were both in deep slumber. They were so alike in some respects, she so pretty even in this bedraggled state, and his pale, yet handsome features. That fine moustache above his lips…with an effort, she resisted the urge to rush toward him.

He was Sela's heart and soul. The memory of her treachery returned to torment her, and she got slowly to her feet and went outside the bunker with the water canister. She cleaned her face with a palmful of water and drank a little, knowing they must conserve the water and food Thabo had procured, until he should return with more.

If only the yak herder would come back here quickly, with the Khempo. That was all she wanted, she told herself, to unite Jaswant and Sela with the blessings of the lama. After that, there would be no more to do in life, for her. She cared not whether the yak herder wanted her or not.

That was when she heard the sounds. She listened, carefully. Rushing to a spot in the trenches from where she could get a panoramic view of the road below, she listened again. Now she could make out the faint, crunching sounds. Was that the noise of heavy wheels on rock, the growling of machinery? Maybe…maybe it was…an army on the road.

It might be the Chinese. Maybe they were on the move…

She hurried back to the bunker, to find that Sela was awake and feeding Jaswant out of the food in the satchel. He ate hungrily, and it appeared that he was going to doze off again.

'We must leave this place,' said Noora, 'Quickly!'

Sela glanced at her, but went on feeding him.

'Do you hear me? We have to go. Escape…'

At this Jaswant fixed his gaze upon Noora, and her heart

quailed. But there was no indication in his eyes that he recalled anything of their recent intimacy. But then, he hadn't known it was her. She hardly mattered to him.

She did not know whether she was hurt or grateful. Sela wasn't even looking in her direction, having eyes only for her lover, who had been delivered miraculously into her hands.

'Find out where they are...how far away...'

Jaswant was speaking to her. Without a word, or looking at him, Noora went out of the bunker once more. She climbed on the mule and let it follow the narrow trail down from the knoll towards the road below, but instead of approaching the road, where any Chinese might see her if they were in the vicinity, she took another track parallel to the highway, and far enough above it for her to travel unseen.

A half hour later, she was perched within hailing distance of a major encampment of the Chinese. Blue caps were everywhere. So were large guns, vehicles and a concourse of animals and slaves. Clearly, this army was preparing to move.

Turning around, she urged the mule to go faster and faster, and goaded by apprehension, she was back at the trio's secure location atop the knoll in far less time than it had taken her on the way down.

'The Chinese,' she blurted out, stumbling into the bunker, 'They're on their way. They will be here soon.'

Sela looked at her sister now, fear writ large in her eyes. Then, she turned to Jaswant, 'We must leave...quickly...my love...'

'We are going nowhere,' he said, his voice still barely more than a whisper, but resolute. 'Help me stand up...'

'No...wait! You are badly hurt,' protested Sela. Perceiving her sister's confusion, and Jaswant's quiet determination, Noora hurried forward and helped Jaswant to his feet.

'Take me outside,' he said, ignoring Sela's protests and hand wringing.

Once outside in the sun, he stood blinking for a while, getting his eyes used to the bright sunlight, clearing his head. Then, with one arm thrown about Sela's shoulder, he walked slowly forward pointing to the trench, which ran the width of the cliff top where they were ensconced. 'We will set up the MMG inside that bunker…there. And the rifles…we can fire from the trenches…there…and there…'

'But why?' Sela asked, still spooning warm rum into his mouth as he went about implementing his plan. 'Why must we stay back in this desolation? We have a mule. You can ride, and we sisters will walk. If you don't wish to join your comrades at Se La Pass… I know of a trail that will take us back home… avoiding the Chinese.'

He paused and stood for a moment looking at her, arms akimbo. Then he turned and gathered her in his arms. He kissed her eyes, brows and chin, afterwards pressing his lips to hers for a long while, until she went quite limp in his embrace.

Noora was busy trying to drag the MMG into position as Jaswant had indicated. Yet, she was aware of the intimacy between her sister and the man she…no! Once more, she pushed that sinful thought firmly out of her mind.

Under Jaswant's direction, the girls cleaned the rifles. Then he made them practise loading and unloading the magazines, and firing…without bullets, of course. When, at last, he was quite satisfied with the positioning of all the weapons, he entered the bunker and hefted the machine gun. At a gesture from him, Sela handed him the ammo belt. Fitting this into the breech of the MMG and clapping his eyes to the gun sight, he looked down the barrel into the distance, gauging range and the gun's alignment.

'How long can we wait here?' Sela asked him. 'We will run out of food, soon. You need rest, and more food.'

He gazed at her and smiled, as if to say, 'I need only you by my side.'

She sighed and shook her head, then went back to the bunker to fetch the food and liquor that Noora had been warming on the impromptu stove she had conjured up with some stones, sticks and matches.

As Sela carried the food and drink to her Jaswant, Noora started to patrol the periphery of the feature they were occupying, her eyes riveted on the road below while her ears tried to shut out the sounds of the conversation between her sister...and Jaswant.

Sela was sitting beside him in the trench, with one arm thrown about him.

'I must smell awful, don't I?' he grinned. 'So do you, my darling. I wonder when I took a bath...last. When this is over, let us find a waterfall and stand together under the cold water... quite naked...'

She could not understand most of what he said in his native Garhwali, but she giggled and hugged him, as though she did. Placing her head on his shoulder, she breathed deep of his aroma.

The patter of soft, quick feet broke their embrace. It was Noora, peering into the bunker.

'They are here,' she said, quite simply, and walked hurriedly off to man one of the rifles, as Jaswant had taught them.

He now pushed Sela gently away and pointed, 'Go, and help your sister with her rifle. After she fires all the rounds in the magazine, load it for her like I taught you...' With that, he climbed out of the bunker and hastened to man the other rifle at the far end of the defensive trench.

Sela saw her sister lift the rifle butt into the hollow beneath her collarbone in the manner he had trained them to, and she shuddered and closed her eyes.

Now she heard the sounds, too. The Chinese were on the march.

A short while later, Sela rose out of the trench and peered down at the road below. 'But they…they will go past us!' she called to him, 'We are safe here.'

'We must not let them…pass.'

'But…why?' Sela's heart sank, and her eyes became moist again. 'Why…'

Already, he was squinting down the sights of his rifle, at the moving mass in the distance. 'We must stop them here for as long as we can. That is the job of a defender. That is the job my platoon was given…and…'A' Company…' even before his words trailed off his finger took up the slack on the trigger and the rifle began to speak. He fired rapidly, with the accuracy and expertise of a professional soldier.

Immediately, on the road below, Noora and Sela saw blue-capped figures dropping.

Howls of surprise and shouted commands reached their ears.

A couple of minutes later, seemingly after the Chinese had overcome the shock of this unexpected attack, a retaliatory volley was hurled at the defenders.

'Keep your head down!' Jaswant called to the girls, and they crouched in the trench as shells thudded into the hillside below or flew far above their heads.

When the Chinese response ceased, Jaswant picked up his rifle and began to fire again. The enemy soldiers, trying to climb the hillside, were sitting ducks. More of them fell to his bullets.

There were more shouts from the Chinese below, and this time the retaliatory fire lasted several minutes.

Meanwhile, Jaswant had moved into the bunker and was squinting through the sights of the MMG. The defenders could see more blue caps starting up the hill.

'Now, Noora!' yelled Jaswant, 'Fire!'

Noora, already on edge, tugged at her rifle's trigger, and although she had never fired a weapon before and the butt of the rifle slammed back into her shoulder like a mule's kick, she had the gratification of seeing one of the enemy fall.

'Good for you, Noora,' Jaswant called, 'You got one. You... Sela! Reload the other rifle like I showed you!'

Noora continued to pump bullets, one by one, in the direction of the advancing Chinese. Most of them missed their mark. Sela was fumbling with the rifle Jaswant had emptied, and she somehow managed to reload it.

At that moment, Jaswant squeezed the trigger of the MMG. The machine gun spat death at the Chinese below. His deadly accurate fire wreaked havoc in their ranks.

There were screams of terror as the enemy ran for their lives, or fell, riddled with bullets. Now there was pandemonium in the Chinese ranks.

'Stay down,' said Jaswant, gesturing, and just as the sisters ducked into the trench the Chinese heavy artillery thundered again. This time the response was long and relentless. Mortar shells and rifle fire echoed and re-echoed, shattering rock and splattering clods of earth all about the hillside, until it seemed the entire hill would dissolve under that pounding.

However, the trio on the knoll were beyond reach of the enemy's weapons, at least for the time being.

Jaswant crawled out of the bunker, and sat panting on the grass outside, clearly exhausted from the effort. Sela rushed towards him, alarmed.

'Stop!' he called, weakly, 'Tell Noora...to stop! They're retreating... They're falling back... Don't waste bullets...'

Even before his words trailed off, the soldier had slumped on the grassy slope.

# 22

Senior Captain Xie was livid. Already disappointed by the loss of two young, good-looking Monpa girls—he was sick of compliant Chinese women who always treated him with deference, and treated sex like a chore—the officer had thought matters could hardly get worse. He was lying in bed trying to take a nap, tossing and turning, wondering at the unexpected twists his vision for the future was taking, when the message arrived from headquarters.

'Reach Se La immediately,' the brusque message from the Colonel read.

In the first place, the order to march had come at the wrong time. Xie was going to consult with his subordinates in the morning. He was not ready to move his troops, yet. Those Garhwalis had inflicted some heavy casualties on his unit. Two of his finest officers had died in the battle for the open ground in the Nuranang valley, before the Indians retreated inexplicably.

However, now that the order to march had been received, he was resolved to display his true mettle. He would show that stuck-up Colonel what material he, Senior Captain Xie, was made of.

'It should take us at least twenty-four hours to arrive in

Se La, with all our men and materials,' his 2i/c said, looking anxious.

'We will climb that pass within six hours!' Xie barked. 'I will personally shoot dead anyone who holds us back. Is that clear?'

That was in the morning. Now, at 1400 hours, the Regiment was stalled. The attack on his troops had come out of the blue, literally. At first the Chinese, lulled into complacency by their knowledge that there were no enemy troops left anywhere before Se La, assumed that the Indians had left behind a lone sniper.

He was on a promontory to the right of the Se La road, and had the drop on Xie's troops. Still, he was only one man with a gun, and the regiment's crack troops would deal with the sniper in a matter of minutes.

But when the bullets rained down upon the Chinese, from different locations on that high rock, Xie began to have misgivings. One man could not fire that many bullets, and from so many different directions. Had the Indians left behind a platoon to harass his army?

Two attempts to storm the hill had failed, with a dozen casualties.

His six hours were already up, Xie realized, and he was nowhere nearer getting to Se La Pass. This delay would only provide that snob of a Colonel with another chance to rub Xie's nose in the dust. He had no doubt that the CO would welcome this opportunity to tell his superiors at the PLA High Command, 'I told you so! That Xie...he doesn't deserve to be Senior Captain...'

The Chinese cannon opened up now, trying to knock the Indians off the feature. But they were firing uphill and at an impossible angle. The difficulty was that with their artillery going, the Chinese infantry also could not advance up the slope; they ran the risk of getting caught in the crossfire and falling to their own shells even if they did escape the enemy's bullets.

Still, the guns kept up the pressure, with the result that after a couple of hours of relentless battering all seemed quiet on the hilltop.

'I think that's done for them, Sir,' announced an officer, marching up to Xie and saluting. 'Not a peep out of them, now…' he had barely finished speaking when a sudden, metallic chatter shattered the silence on the hillside. The MMG on the hill was spitting insults, again.

Xie glared at the officer, who backpedalled hastily and then turned and sprinted away, not even waiting to see his Senior Captain's reaction.

'How many men have we lost?' Xie asked the officer who brought him a report as night began to fall on the Jang-Se La road.

The officer hesitated, seeing his superior's menacing glance, and then almost whispered, 'Maybe fifty… could be more… Sir…'

Fifty men! Losing that many of the PLA's finest soldiers in one day's action, against probably a section strength of defenders, platoon at the most—Xie could almost visualize the Colonel's nose curling in disgust at his subordinate's presumed inefficiency.

Thabo still could not believe that he was doing this. Here he was, urging his mule through dark, trackless mountains and culverts, trying to hide from the Chinese, when, in fact, he should have been in the good books of the victorious invaders.

What had gone wrong, he wondered, that he should have

lost his leverage with the Chinese. If only he had stuck to his original plan, and kept his dealings with them on strictly business lines, providing supplies and porters to them, he might have been sitting pretty in Tawang, calling the shots. There was no knowing what heights he could have attained once the war was over and the Chinese had become rulers of all this territory. He might even have gone on to become one of their principal agents dealing with the cowardly Indian government and its military minions.

Instead, here he was chaperoning the Khempo of the great monastery through this dangerous wilderness, for some obscure reason that he could not even understand. He grumbled under his breath, careful not to let his pious companion get wind of his real feelings about this mad adventure.

The Khempo had initially been sceptical when Thabo told him about Noora's request. But when he told him a partial truth, that she was in Chinese custody and her life might be in danger if he did not do as the Chinese officer directed, which was to fetch a lama to solemnize his marriage to Noora, the holy man consented and set out with the yak herder.

They were now at the remaining bridge across the Tawang Chu. Thabo knew the crossing was under Chinese control, and although he did not wish to hazard crossing the bridge, they had to take the chance. He himself was used to climbing and crossing the high mountains and the jungle streams regularly, and if he were alone, he might have avoided the Chinese. But the Khempo was a liability, in that respect.

The two men were urging their mules across the bridge when the Chinese sentries accosted them. Thabo being in a yak herder's getup might have got through without difficulty, but the lama was another matter. To make matters worse, the ascetic had refused to don a herder or slave's garb for the journey.

'Where are you going at this hour?' snarled one of the two sentries on the far side of the bridge, after Thabo and his companion had managed to get that far. 'And what do you want...'

'I...Sir, as you see I am a yak herder, and I've been supplying meat to the great Chinese masters,' said Thabo, trying to sound as obsequious as possible.

'I can see you are...you stink like one!' snapped the sentry, and he and his colleague laughed aloud at this wisecrack.

Thabo tried to smile, to humour them so that they would create no trouble.

'We are going to my broke at Se La pass,' said Thabo quickly, 'I have several head of cattle there that I must deliver to the victorious armies of China...'

'Se La?' demanded the sentry, his eyes gleaming with suspicion. 'But what is this priest doing with you, eh? He doesn't look like a herder?'

'Just look at his clothes,' said the other sentry, lining his rifle at the Khempo, 'What are you doing here, man of god?'

For a moment, Thabo's heart stopped beating, and he thought all was lost. He knew that the Chinese hated monks more than anyone else, whether Tibetan or Monpa.

'Wait...' Thabo started forward, at which the Khempo stopped him with a gesture.

'I am going with this good man,' said the monk with perfect equanimity, 'To conduct a marriage, my son.'

'Marriage?' the sentries looked at one another, 'What marriage...whose...'

'Haven't you heard? A Chinese military officer is taking to wife a Monpa girl who is related to this young man here...and he fetched me along so that I might solemnize the wedding.

That is all there is to it.'

'Yes, yes!' Thabo almost shouted, marvelling at the old lama's presence of mind, and the wisdom of his decision to tell the Khempo a half-truth, 'A marriage cannot happen among our people without a lama, you see? That is why the great Captain Xie directed me to fetch the Khempo from the monastery. Now do you understand? Please do not delay us any longer, or the Captain will be angry with me…' and he closed with a murmur, 'and with you…'

For a moment more, the sentries stood undecided, exchanging glances, and then one of them whispered to his colleague, 'It is true the Captain has a Monpa girl with him… even two, I have heard rumours. So, we had better not…'

As Thabo and the Khempo left the sentries behind and urged their mules into motion, the yak herder resolved that he would seek the monk's forgiveness for the deception, once they were safely away from the Chinese.

Meanwhile, high up in the hills fringing the road, a four-legged traveller sniffed the air. He caught the faint scent of mules, at a fair distance below where he was perched on a rock. It was a risk, going that far down from his mountain redoubt, where he might encounter human beings, his greatest enemy. He had not forgotten his recent encounter with a couple of them, which had resulted in his being deprived of a reasonable meal. But he was famished, not having eaten anything for over a day and night. Food was hard to come by, with the sounds of explosions through the past few days and nights having scared most of his natural prey away from these mountains, and he was now willing to try anything to fill his growling belly.

# 23

That night was no less difficult for the defenders of the Se La road, despite their success in keeping the Chinese down for an entire day.

Exhausted with his efforts of the day, Jaswant slept almost the sleep of the dead, and the sisters took turns, one watching over him while the other patrolled the fringes of their defensive position, just in case the enemy decided to climb the hill after sunset.

Fortunately for them, the Chinese appeared to harbour no such plans. They had probably lost the stomach for a fight, after the pasting of the day.

'They will come again...' murmured Noora to her sister, 'If not this evening, at daybreak tomorrow. One of us will have to stay up through the night.'

Sela was spooning some of the remaining soup into Jaswant's mouth, little by little so that he might not choke on the warm liquid. Noora had put a bandage over his head wound, containing a poultice she made out of some herbs growing in the thickets nearby.

'Let us put him on the mule and leave this place, sister,' Sela said at one point. If somehow they could take him home to Tawang—although the place was now almost a day and a half's journey away, considering they would have to travel slowly given his condition—they would be able to care for him better.

Noora shook her head, 'No, the Chinese are all over the place. We must wait here for as long as we can...'

The sisters went about their respective chores, one watching for any enemy activity and the other caring for the convalescent. The night was far advanced, when Sela said again, to her sister, 'Maybe the Chinese will go away in the darkness, since we are not firing at them...'

'Never! Over...my body...'

The sisters were taken aback to see that it was Jaswant speaking. He was awake now, probably revived by the rest and the nutrition Sela had been plying him with.

Noora hid her relief, at this development. All this while, she had been praying that Thabo would return soon with the Khempo, so that she might be able to complete the one significant duty that remained for her to perform. This was also the reason she had not been keen on leaving this place, knowing Thabo with his tracking skills would find his way here, and if they left this place he would be confused, and might go on to Se La pass, thinking they had moved in that direction.

'Now that Jaswant is awake, I will pray for a while,' she said to her sister.

Sela looked at her, shaking her head, 'What has prayer ever given you, sister?'

Noora gazed quietly back, in the gloom of the bunker, and Sela wished she had not said that to her. Holding out one hand, she squeezed Noora's fingers, as if to express remorse.

After Noora left the bunker to go out into the open and

meditate, Jaswant sat slowly up and said to Sela, 'Help me into the trench…I wish to see what is going on out there…'

'No!' she protested, 'You're not well, and I cannot let you go out there. It is too cold.'

'If Noora can be out in the cold at this hour, I can, too. I am a soldier.'

'No one doubts your courage…but you must remain alive in order to fight tomorrow.'

'What if the Chinese sneak up on us in the night?' he asked, getting slowly to his feet, so that she hastened to help him. 'We will all be dead then, and there will be no tomorrow.'

'I don't care about tomorrow…if I can be with you now…'

He shook his head, 'Now that I have found you, I am not willing to die.'

Taking off her blue Tibetan coat, she threw it over his shoulders, before helping him into the trench. There they sat, trying to peer into the darkness to detect any movement in the rocky, thicket-strewn slopes running away from the hilltop to the road far below.

Noora sat hunched a short distance away, meditating.

Not a leaf stirred, no insects chirped in the cold night, and the Chinese, it seemed, were as apprehensive of the unpredictable enemy perched high above them, as the trio were of their enemies' intentions. A restless quiet had descended upon this unlikely battlefield.

Sometime later, a gentle breeze stirred the hilltop, rocking the watchers, lulling their senses. No one knew when they were carried away in the arms of sleep that night.

It was well past dawn when one of the exhausted sentinels stirred, woken by the sudden cacophony of birds.

Waking with a start, Noora found that they had all slept

through the night. A quick glance told her Sela and Jaswant had fallen asleep inside the trench. She went across to check whether Jaswant was well, that his wound had not opened or bled during the night. But he seemed to be resting peacefully, as was her sister.

Then she rushed to the edge of the bluff and peered carefully down the hillside. She thought something stirred. She jumped into the trench and picked up her rifle. Checking to make sure the magazine was full, she locked it and lifted the rifle to her shoulder. Again, there was a stirring on the slope, and she thought she saw a splash of blue. The rifle bucked in her hands, and a bullet shattered the quiet of the morning.

There was an immediate reaction from below, and warning shouts followed by a volley of gunfire crashing into the hillside.

By now Sela and Jaswant were awake.

'Quick, get me a little water to wash my face…help me to the bunker!' he urged Sela.

Noora waited until the Chinese stopped firing, and then emptied her magazine slowly, deliberately into the slopes below. A scream of agony told her some of the bullets had struck home.

Jaswant was already at the MMG. 'Sela, help me load this,' he called.

The young girl sprinted toward the bunker, and the Chinese were just beginning their upward movement again, when the machine gun began to spit death once more. Jaswant swivelled the gun on its tripod, raking the slopes, inch by inch. He knew that he was short of ammunition. He had to make every shot count, if possible.

The effect of Jaswant's reply was devastating. As the enemy scattered to the four directions, leaving their dead and their wounded, Noora's bullets followed them, dropping dead a couple of the Chinese in their precipitate flight.

Given a choice, the leopard would not have hunted in daylight. But this was a crisis. He was almost starving, and there was no knowing when another such opportunity would present itself, if he let this quarry go. Now he could smell the humans also, with the mules. One of them had a powerful odour of raw meat that the predator found irresistible.

Thabo was careful to travel on a course parallel to the main road below, so that he would not lose his way. He knew where he had left Noora, and that she was probably waiting on the raised bluff at some height from the spot where they had met. That was the best position in this area, from where one could watch the road, and anyone approaching.

His present course would take him and his companion in the direction of that very hilltop, even though it meant going through some gullies, and a barely visible mithun trail lined on both sides and often choked by thickets. To their left and beyond a line of thickets screening them was the rock strewn, grassy slope undulating to the road below. Above and to the travellers' right were several series of tall rocks interspersed with thickets. They seemed to continue interminably into the distance.

As the two riders swayed on the sure-footed mules, pressing steadily toward their destination, the herder tried not to think of what he might find, once they reached the place. Noora would be waiting…and who else? Was Sela there…and him? That…Indian!

Why had Noora asked him to bring the Khempo along? He wished now that he had not listened to her. Deep inside him, though, was the still-flickering hope that Sela also would be there, waiting. Maybe not for him...but she might be there. On the other hand, if the Indian was already dead, killed in the battle...but then, why the lama?

Several times already, they had heard the sound of gunfire. What did that signify? The Indian battalions were supposed to have withdrawn to Se La. Who then were the Chinese firing at? A sneaking fear entered Thabo's mind. Was it...could it be? But no, that was impossible! How could one soldier, or even a few, fight an army?

All this speculation was too much for the yak herder's slow, lumbering thought process, accustomed more to the proclivities of the animals he reared than human beings. He raised his eyes momentarily toward the sun, shielding his eyes with one hand from the blazing white light reflecting off the rocks.

At that very moment, a faint stirring behind the rocks above and to their right caught the herder's eye. For all his mediocre intellect, he was a man of the outdoors, and an expert tracker and hunter. In the instant that his eyes detected the movement, his brain registered the threat.

As the leopard came shooting out of the rocks upon the quarry below, Thabo was already twisting in his seat, the machete out and describing a sweeping arc through the air. The beast's claws were within striking distance when the wicked steel wielded by Thabo's powerful arm caught it in the neck. The carnivore's roars and the herder's snarls mixed in a terrible, fearsome medley of sound.

But, although the machete sliced through the beast's skin and bone, the momentum of his charge was such that the furry body thudded into Thabo, unseating him and sending him tumbling down the hillside.

Spooked by the leopard's attack, the Khempo's mule also went ratcheting downhill. The animal slithered and stumbled after the herder's falling body, and minutes later, men and mule and cat had landed in a growling, howling, flailing mess at the bottom of the slope, right in the middle of a group of alarmed Chinese.

It was only because one of the soldiers happened to have seen Thabo earlier and recognized him as the herder who brought meat, churpi and salt to their camp in Tawang that the Chinese did not shoot the prisoners out of hand.

'We'd better take him to the Senior Captain,' said this man. 'He should be told...'

The prisoners were hauled without ado before the battalion commander. As soon as Xie set eyes on the herder, his first instinct was to whip out his pistol and fill the intruder with lead. But even as he aligned his weapon at the man, the Captain's eyes sized up the other captive.

'A monk!' he sneered, 'What are you doing here...where were the two of you going?'

Since Thabo had confessed the sin of his lie to the lama after they escaped the sentries at the bridge, even the Khempo now knew better than to speak to the Chinese Captain.

'I am going to have you skinned like a yak, alive, if your tongues don't start wagging quickly!' threatened the Captain.

When neither of the prisoners spoke, Xie was so incensed that his right hand crashed against the lama's cheek. The holy man went reeling.

'You...you can't hit the Khempo!' shouted Thabo.

'Oh, so you value this dog's life, do you? Now...you better tell me what you were doing here, Monpa slaves and cowards, before I lose patience and have you killed and stuffed with hay...'

'I should have done that to those two Monpa girls too,' he went on, 'after raping them. I would have given them to my soldiers to play with…and then fed them to the dogs…'

At this insult, the dam of the herder's anger broke, and he thundered, 'You…it is you who are cowards! I know that the Indians have stopped you here. One…one man and a couple of girls have thrashed your great army. You know who that man is on that mountain there? He…he is a great warrior…a great wrestler…'

As his emotion subsided, the enormity of what he had said dawned upon Thabo, and he saw a cunning gleam come into the Senior Captain's eyes. 'Oh, so that is what is going on, is it? One…man…two girls?'

Xie turned and barked orders rapidly, at which a couple of soldiers grabbed the Khempo and dragged him out of the commander's tent.

'Now you listen to me, yak herder,' hissed Xie, his eyes boring through Thabo's heavy, sleep-deprived eyelids, 'I am not going to have you skinned alive…it is that holy man of yours…that dog of a Monpa priest who will be punished…if you don't…'

# 24

Noora lifted the canister to place water on the fire to boil, so that she might make a little more soup. Peering into the container, she realized there was very little left, at the bottom of the can.

They were running out of meat, too. This might be the last meal they could partake of, until Thabo returned. She presumed he would have the sense to bring some food with him.

Considering the state of their rations, Noora gave most of the soup to Jaswant, and kept a little for Sela and herself. The remaining meat she distributed between them, telling Sela when she enquired, 'Yes, of course…I've a bit of meat for myself, too.'

Sela was too enrapt in her lover's well-being at the moment, it seemed, to care too much about her sister. In any case, Noora had always been the provider at home, the mother figure who looked after her younger sibling and her father. The old man would enquire about her welfare occasionally, while Sela was caught up in her pranks, and ate ravenously of whatever was provided by Noora, without ever asking whether her sister too had eaten.

Noora didn't mind, of course. It had been her responsibility to look after her father and sister then, and at the moment she had to keep these two in good fettle. All through her chores of preparing the soup and meat, she kept mumbling her prayers.

The Chinese hadn't returned after their early morning attempt had failed, thanks to Noora's waking up just in time.

As the day stretched on, the hill was bathed in glorious sunshine.

It was late afternoon, when Jaswant asked Noora, 'Get me a little water…to wash my eyes and face. I cannot see clearly.'

She gave him some of the remaining water to wash his face, and a little to drink. All the liquid that remained was the few millilitres of diluted rum in the bottle, which Sela would slip occasionally between Jaswant's lips to keep him warm.

When the Chinese grew venturesome again, it was close to evening. This time, they came in several waves, probably hoping to overwhelm the defenders by sheer weight of numbers. They might have realized also that the people on the knoll would be running out of food and ammunition, sooner or later.

For close to an hour, the atmosphere around that lonely hill feature in Nuranang reverberated with massive explosions and the incessant chatter of gunfire.

But if the attackers hoped to intimidate Jaswant, they were mistaken. Having rested for several hours, he was almost his usual self now, and able to stand up by himself and man the MMG and the rifles. By now, the girls also had grown accustomed to the rifles. The defenders' fire was, therefore, that much more lethal.

The Chinese show of strength didn't seem to have worked. When they withdrew that evening, the invaders left behind several scores of their comrades on the slopes and in gullies reticulating the face of that hill.

'That's done for them this evening,' Jaswant slumped on the

floor of the bunker, having been on his feet for over an hour, manning the MMG. 'I don't think they will return.'

Once more Sela said to him, 'Give up this obstinacy, Jaswant. You have proved that you are the bravest of the brave. But I do not want to lose you again. Let us go home...or even to Se La pass to join your comrades, if that is what you wish.'

Noora had just brought him the last bit of meat, which she had saved, and she heard Sela's words. She paused at the door of the bunker, as if to hear his reply.

'What do you think, Noora...let me ask you. You are wisest among the three of us. Do you think we will leave this place alive?'

She heard his question, but did not turn or look at either of them. Without a word she left the bunker, and made her way to one of the rifles positioned at the edge of the trench.

After a while, exhausted and starving, Noora fell asleep, still holding the rifle. Sometime during that night, Jaswant walked over to where the elder sister was slumped in the trench, gently snoring, and draped the blue Tibetan coat over her shoulders.

Returning to Sela, he kissed her brows and said, 'We have one another to keep ourselves warm...'

She yawned and giggled, and held him close.

❦

For the first time in his life, probably, the yak herder prayed with feeling. As his lips mumbled the words of almost forgotten verses, his mind tried frantically to recall the benevolent face of the Sakya Muni.

But all he could visualize was the scowling visage of the Chinese officer who sat on the mule behind, his vengeful eyes not wavering even for a moment from the bulky figure of the yak herder riding the leading animal. Apart from the pistol at his hip, Xie carried in his right hand an automatic rifle with bayonet fixed, and held on to the mule's halter with his left.

Thabo wished he hadn't listened to Noora. He also prayed that if at all there was anyone on the hilltop, it should be that blasted Indian soldier who had made his life a living hell. He prayed that Noora and Sela were far, far away, preferably back home in Tawang.

But as the mountain-savvy mules picked their way along the almost invisible mithun track running between the rhododendron hedges and rocky outcrops, he realized it was a vain hope. He knew the kind of woman Noora was. She would be waiting. Well…maybe Sela wasn't there…?

The Chinese Captain had taken Thabo's advice of venturing up the hill close to dawn, so that they could catch the people on the knoll unawares. It is darkest at that hour, and people tend to be in very deep sleep, Thabo had told the man, who had nodded approvingly. He knew all that, of course. He was an officer of the PLA.

Daylight might have exposed them to the risk of being seen and shot down. At that distance, the defenders wouldn't know that Thabo was one of the climbers, and would shoot at anything that moved.

'Although you are a stupid yak herder, your suggestion makes sense,' growled Xie, 'If we can capture those Indians up there, I shall let you go…and that monk of yours. But if you try any tricks…remember that I will be right behind you, with this bayonet ready…'

Still, Thabo had the wild hope that he might somehow be able to shake off the Chinese as soon as they gained the hilltop, and overwhelm his tormentor with the help of the girls and

Jaswant, if at all they were waiting up there.

The first birds had begun to chirp as the riders closed in on their objective.

The yak herder had guessed that the defenders would be facing the road below, and so he had taken an approach, albeit an extremely difficult one, which had forced them to climb steeply first, but would have enabled them to come down upon the defensive position from the rear, provided no further obstacle had been laid in their path.

Orange was already tinging the eastern sky beyond the far mountains, when Thabo's mule broke through a particularly dense thicket of rhododendrons. At the very moment that his trained eyes settled on the human figure in a blue coat sitting hunched at the far side of the flat, grassy hilltop, his mule cantered forward, its hooves clattering on the rock beneath. The figure rose instantaneously at the sudden sound and he saw, even in that gloom, that it was Noora.

'Thabo!' his name broke from her lips, tinged with relief and surprise. 'Tha…'

But then, her eyes glimpsed another figure on a mule breaking out of the thicket from where the yak herder had emerged. Even as Thabo's mule rushed towards her, she had the presence of mind to yell, 'Jaswant! Jaswant!'

Having rested for a large part of the previous day, the soldier had only just dozed off, when the intruders appeared. At Noora's call, the warrior's every instinct came rapidly, instantaneously alive, and he leaped out of the trench on the far side, where he and Sela had been on watch.

Simultaneously, the Chinese snapped on a flashlight, so that Jaswant's figure was bathed in its harsh glare. But as Jaswant started to bring the rifle to bear upon the flashlight wielding enemy, he heard a sudden rustling behind him, and Sela's figure flew right past and towards the onrushing attacker.

Down and forward, the Chinese on the mule stabbed with the bayonet, meaning to impale the Indian with his weapon. But Sela's unexpected rush spoilt his calculations, and it was the girl's chest that bore the brunt of his attack. The polished, heavy steel sliced though the young woman's breast, and she slumped forward, with a sigh. As she fell, her weight dragged Xie's rifle down, and with it the man holding the weapon.

'Se...la!' yelled Jaswant, 'Sela!' Mad with grief and rage, he came bounding out of the trench, throwing aside the rifle to hold her in his arms. But the Chinese had recovered from the fall. With a howl of rage, Xie launched himself at Jaswant.

Instinctively, Jaswant adopted the role of the wrestler he was. The men went into a clinch. They pushed and pulled, roaring like lions, each trying to get a grip on his adversary. Then they pounded one another with their fists. Jaswant's wound had started to bleed, but he paid no attention. All he saw was the sneering face of this demon that had stabbed his Sela.

With a sudden feint, he slipped inside his enemy's grasping arms and caught the man's neck in a powerful grip. The Chinese groaned and writhed, while Jaswant squeezed, tighter and tighter, until his enemy's body went limp. Then he switched his grip, and with an almighty effort, he raised Xie's body high up in the air and slammed it into the ground.

Noora and Thabo had been watching this tableau in fear and horror. Neither of them could move, nor could they intervene in this life and death struggle.

Then the sound of several, scurrying feet came from the rhododendron brushes, and Thabo realized instantly that they were Chinese soldiers. They rushed towards Jaswant, who was grieving over his Sela.

In one, quick movement Thabo swept Noora up in his arms, dumped her on the mule and swung himself onto the saddle. As more Chinese broke through the thickets, the sound of the mule's galloping hooves rang out, aloud, under the pale, chill sky of the mountains.

# 25

For a long while after Mrs Ralte finished telling her story, no one spoke a word.

When Akash spoke, presently, feeling obliged to break the silence since this retelling of a legend had been arranged for his benefit, he tried to inject his words with the required deference, while not seeming to be too credulous. That was his brief, after all.

'That is quite a story, Sir…er…Ma'am,' he said, 'I feel honoured that you chose to share this with me.'

The elderly woman looked at him with kindness in her eyes, and at the same time, there was something else in her eyes which seemed to tell him that she could look into his inmost depths, and sense what he was thinking. But it was her husband that she addressed, 'Take me home, now. It is getting cold, and I am not as sprightly as I used to be.'

She walked slowly away, down the slope along the now neatly paved path lined by white painted bricks, leading to the memorial and the road below.

The Gram Pradhan turned to Akash, saying, 'You must excuse me, Lieutenant. We are old people, you see. I hope the time spent with us has been rewarding, Sir…'

'You cannot imagine how much,' said the Lieutenant, shaking hands with the official, 'If you don't mind we will stay back for a while at this place...you understand...?'

'Of course, of course,' said Mr Ralte amiably as he moved off. His wife had turned around, and was calling to him to hurry up.

'Coming, Rincin!' he shouted back, 'Coming...'

As the village official hurried down the path, Akash turned to his orderly, 'What do you think, eh?'

'I think, Sir...,' the Lance Naik saluted and barked, '*Jai Badri Vishaal*!'

❦

Akash was in his office reading a day-old newspaper, the next morning, when his orderly entered with a cup of tea. As he placed the steaming cup on his officer's table and turned to leave, the Lieutenant said, 'Did you take Mr Ralte's...er...the telephone number of the Gram Pradhan's residence?'

'I did, Saabji!' said the Lance Naik with alacrity, fishing out his cell phone. 'Do you wish to speak with him, Saabji? Shall I dial the number?'

'No. Just give it to me.' Akash saved the number in his handset.

After a while, when he had finished the tea and had read the newspaper, he dialled the number his orderly had given him. As he expected, it was a woman who came on the line, almost immediately.

'This is Lieutenant Akash Sinha,' he spoke in English, out of habit, and then hastily followed up in Hindi, 'Ma'am...you remember me?'

'I do remember, Lieutenant Akash,' Mrs Ralte said, in English, 'What is it that I can do for you, Sir?'

'Er...well...' he was taken aback, slightly, at her flawless diction, 'I...I was wondering...can I come over and talk to you, Ma'am. Alone?'

'When do you wish to come over, Lieutenant?'

'Right away...'

Mrs Ralte welcomed Akash into her home, and first served him tea and a snack, before she sat down on another sofa facing him, 'Yes...?'

For a moment he gazed at her, wondering where to begin, then said abruptly, 'You did go to school in Delhi after all, didn't you?'

She nodded, gravely, 'And college, afterwards. My father retired from the Ministry of Home Affairs, many years ago.'

His eyes darted to a large, framed photograph kept on top of a bookcase standing against the wall behind her. 'Those... are your children, Mrs Ralte?'

'Yes...my son and my daughter. They study at the University of Delhi.' A smile flitted across her face, 'and you may call me Rincin if you wish...'

'Oh, no,' he shook his head quickly, 'That would be presumptuous of me, Ma'am...'

'Very well, Lieutenant Akash,' she inclined her head, and now her features were grave, 'But you did not come here to enquire about my family, did you?'

'Er...well, no, actually. The thing is, Ma'am...I suppose you understand. A story...like this...needs to be backed by some documentary proof,' he hesitated, 'You know how our bureaucracy works...'

She nodded, getting to her feet, 'Of course, I do. As I said, my father was a government official. Please give me a minute, will you...'

Then she went into the house, while Akash remained seated on the edge of the sofa, fidgeting and wondering what he had let himself in for.

When Mrs Ralte—Rincin—emerged a few minutes later, she had in her hands a large oblong of cellophane. She handed this to him and sat down again, saying, 'Is this what you were looking for, Lieutenant?'

A thrill shot through Akash's bones and the blood pounded in his veins, as he looked at what he was holding. It was a bluish-yellow piece of paper with neat lines of handwritten text. Turning it over, he saw the faded seal of the postal department, and realized this was an inland letter of the type people used, decades ago. The paper was probably crumbling with age, and so protected within the fine cellophane envelope.

He could read Hindi, fortunately. Looking closely at the letter, he still could make out some portions of the text…and the date. November 1962, it said.

'Would you call this documentary proof?' she asked, gently.

He looked up at her, wondering, almost breathless with excitement, 'This…this is incredible…Rincin…er…Ma'am…I… don't know what to say!'

She sat there quietly, gazing at him, waiting for him to speak, until he spoke again, 'I…I can't believe I am holding this…'

'Do you know,' she said, softly, and he thought he saw moisture sparkle in the elderly woman's eyes, 'She…she gave this to me just before she…'

'I…understand,' he didn't know what else to say.

'Sometimes,' she continued as if he hadn't spoken, indeed as if he weren't even in the room at that moment, 'Sometimes when I am reminded of my best friend, I take this out of my old suitcase and look at it…'

Lieutenant Akash Sinha got slowly to his feet. Leaning forward, he placed the cellophane covered document in Mrs Ralte's hands and stood back. Then he saluted.

As she looked up at him he said, 'Some stories...are very personal, Ma'am. It is better that the world doesn't know...'

# Acknowledgements

We gratefully acknowledge the contributions of the following:

Smt. Leelavati Rawat, the martyr's mother, and his family for providing personal information about his life in Dehradun.

Distt. Ex-servicemen's Welfare Board, Dehradun, for helping us trace the Garhwalis' families.

Personnel of the Indian Army at Jaswantgarh, for their inputs regarding the 'Baba'.

Sam Sharma (last known email aksh9@airtelmail.in), for early help with the research.

Col. (Retd.) & Smt. Naithani of BEGC (TATRA) Roorkee, who read and endorsed the first draft.

Col. Sanjiv Alipuria (Retd.), for vetting the manuscript.

Late Mr K.C. Verma (IRS, Retd.), who read and critiqued the draft.

Late Mr H.N. Varma (SBI, Retd.), for his encouragement.

Our children, S. Shankar and Rohini, for being our best and worst critics.

Suhail Mathur and The Book Bakers, our agent, without whose enthusiasm and efforts this extraordinary story might not have seen the light of day.

Mr Kapish Mehra and team, for their faith in the 'Baba'.

# Glossary of Hindi/Monpa/Sanskrit/ Tibetan words

| | |
|---|---|
| *apang* | Rice beer, popular among the Monpas |
| *baba* | generally, a holy man, ascetic |
| *banchung* | tiffin box |
| *Basha* | Monpa dwelling, generally of bamboo, wood and stone |
| *bhabhi* | brother's wife |
| *bhaiya* | Brother |
| *Bhawani* | Creative aspect of Durga, the Mother Goddess |
| *Broke* | an animal farm in the high mountains |
| *Brokpa* | a community of herder Monpas |
| *churpi* | cheese made from yak's milk |
| *Darpok* | Coward |
| *dukhang* | the main prayer hall inside a Gompa |
| *Gam Budha* | village head appointed by the local administration |
| *Garhwali* | native of the Garhwal region of Uttarakhand |
| *gompa* | Buddhist temple / shrine |
| *Goral* | a Himalayan species of goat-like ungulate, which is hunted for its flesh and pelt |

| | |
|---|---|
| *Great Monastery* | the Tawang Monastery, the largest Buddhist monastery in India, situated in then Kameng FD (now Tawang district). Also known as Galden Namgyal Lhatse ('the celestial paradise, on a clear night') |
| *Holi mela* | fair/ fete organized during the spring festival of Holi |
| *hoshiyar* | 'On guard!' or 'Be alert!' |
| *Jai Badri Vishaal* | battle cry of the Garhwal Rifles regiment of the Indian Army (invoking the benedictions of Vishnu, the deity at the Badrinath shrine in Chamoli district of Uttarakhand) |
| JCO | Junior Commissioned Officer (such as Subedar Major, Subedar, Naib Subedar/Jemadar. In the Indian Armed forces, officers communicate with soldiers through these JCOs, who have risen from the ranks) |
| *Lhabab Duchen* | Tibetan/ Monpa festival celebrating the descent of the Buddha from Tushita (heaven) |
| *Mithun* | domesticated form of the Indian Bison (Gaur), reared extensively in NE India (Arunachal, |
| *Mohalla* | Nagaland) a quarter/ward of a town or village; a community |
| MMG | Medium Machine Gun (belt fed, tripod mounted, air cooled weapon, of World War vintage) |
| *Namka Chu* | a tributary of the Tawang Chu river in the then Kameng Frontier Division of India's NEFA |
| NCO | Non-Commissioned Officers (such as Lance Naik, Naik and Havildar) are subordinate to the JCOs |
| *Nuranang Chu* | a tributary of the Tawang Chu |
| *Om mani padme hum* | the six-syllable mantra chanted by Buddhists (from the Sanskrit words Mani=jewel and Padma=lotus) |

| | |
|---|---|
| *OR* | Other Ranks (all NCOs and sepoys/ riflemen) |
| *pallang* | bamboo container |
| *prasad* | offering to a deity which is later distributed among devotees |
| *Rinpoche* | Abbot (head) of an order or monastery |
| *Roat* | a sweet dish popular in Garhwal, prepared from whole wheat flour, jaggery, milk, ghee, aniseed and cardamom |
| roti | Chapati |
| *Saabji* | respectful form of address, 'Sir' |
| *sadbhavana* | Goodwill |
| *Sakya Muni* | 'Sage of the Sakyas', a title of Gautama Buddha (he was of the Sakya tribe) |
| *sarkari babu* | government official |
| *Sawaa lakh naal ek ladawaan...* | 'each one of my braves shall be equal to one hundred thousand of the enemy...' (attributed to Gobind Singh, the tenth Guru of the Sikhs) |
| *Sinka* | a type of long gown |
| *Shriman* | an honorific, for men. |
| *Tawang Chu* | major river in Kameng FD |
| *Tomba Sakya Dawa* | The Buddha (Sakya Muni) |
| *Tsopa* | village council |
| *Tushita* | Heaven, where The Buddha and other Bodhisattvas reside (derived from a Sanskrit word) |
| *Urad ki pakori* | a fried savoury made of black lentils |